THE CAT WHO CAME TO BREAKFAST: Peaceful Breakfast Island is turned upside-down by controversy—and murder. Qwill and the cats must find out whodunit . . .

THE CAT WHO BLEW THE WHISTLE: An old steam locomotive has been restored, causing excitement in Moose County. But a murder brings the fun to a screeching halt—and Qwill and Koko are tracking down the culprit . . .

THE CAT WHO SAID CHEESE: The Great Food Explo brings lots of delicious activity to Moose County—as well as a stew of gossip, mystery, and murder . . .

THE CAT WHO TAILED A THIEF: A rash of petty thievery in Pickax puts Qwill and Koko on a killer's elusive trail . . .

THE CAT WHO SANG FOR THE BIRDS: Qwilleran is looking forward to the peaceful beauty of a Moose County spring. Instead, he gets a chorus of noisy birds, a chain of mysterious events—and a bird-calling cat whose fancy has turned to crimesolving . . .

THE CAT WHO SAW STARS: UFOs in Mooseville? With the help of his own little aliens, Qwill investigates the rumors that are flying—but the search for intelligent life turns into a search for a killer . . .

THE CAT WHO WENT UP THE CREEK
Now available in hardcover from G. P. Putnam's Sons

Lilian Jackson Braun

The Cat Who Sniffed Glue

JOVE BOOKS, NEW YORK

This Jove Book contains the complete text of the original hardcover edition. It has been completely reset in a typeface designed for easy reading and was printed from new film.

THE CAT WHO SNIFFED GLUE

A Jove Book / published by arrangement with
the author

PRINTING HISTORY
G. P. Putnam's Sons edition / September 1988
Jove edition / March 1989

The Penguin Putnam Inc. World Wide Web site address is
http://www.penguinputnam.com

ISBN: 0-515-09954-6

A JOVE BOOK®
Jove Books are published by
The Berkley Publishing Group, a division of Penguin Putnam Inc.,
375 Hudson Street, New York, New York 10014.
JOVE and the "J" design are trademarks
belonging to Penguin Putnam Inc.

PROLOGUE

Yes, there really is a place called Moose County, 400 miles north of everywhere. The county seat is Pickax City, population three thousand.

There really is a busboy named Derek Cuttle-brink. And there is a barkeeper who looks like a bear and charges a nickel for a paper napkin. And there is a cat named Kao K'o Kung, who is smarter than people.

If they sound like characters in a play, that's because . . . "All the world's a stage, and all the men and women merely players." So, dim the lights! Raise the curtain!

Act One

SCENE
ONE

Place: A bachelor apartment in Pickax City

Time: Early one morning in late May

Cast: JIM QWILLERAN, former journalist, now heir to the Klingenschoen fortune—a big man, about fifty, with graying hair, bushy moustache and doleful expression

KAO K'O KUNG, a Siamese cat familiarly known as Koko

YUM YUM, another Siamese cat— Koko's constant companion

5

ANDREW BRODIE, Pickax chief of
police

The telephone rang at an early hour, and
Qwilleran reached blindly toward his bedside table.
Half awake, he croaked a hoarse hello and heard an
authoritative voice saying, "I want to talk to you!"

The voice was familiar, but the tone was alarm-
ing. It was Andrew Brodie, the chief of police in
Pickax, and he sounded stern and accusing.

Qwilleran was always groggy before his first cup
of coffee, and his mind groped for an explanation.
Had he put a Canadian nickel in a parking meter?
Tossed an apple core from his car window? Honked
the horn within 500 feet of the hospital?

"Did you hear me? I want to talk to you!" The
tone was not so gruff as before.

Qwilleran was getting his bearings, and he recognized the bantering style that passed for sociability
among adult males in Moose County. "Okay, Brodie," he said. "Do I go to the station and give myself up? Or do you want to send the wagon and
handcuffs?"

"Stay where you are. I'll be right there," said the
chief. "It's about your cat." He hung up abruptly.

Again the possibilities churned in Qwilleran's
mind. Had the Siamese been disturbing the peace?
They were strictly indoor pets, but the male had a
high-decibel yowl and the female had a shriek that
could be duplicated only by a synthesizer. Either of
them could be heard for blocks on a calm day if the

windows were open. It was late May, and the windows were open to admit the sweet refreshing breezes for which Moose County was famous—sweet and refreshing except when they came from the direction of the Kilcally dairy farm.

Hurriedly Qwilleran pulled on some clothes, ran a wet comb through his hair, collected the newspapers cluttering the living room floor, slammed the bedroom door on his unmade bed, and looked out the window in time to see Brodie's police car pulling into the driveway.

Qwilleran lived in an apartment over a four-car garage, formerly the carriage house for the Klingenschoen estate. The carriage house was situated far back on the property; the mansion itself fronted on Main Street facing the park—a huge, square stone building now being remodeled as a theater for stage productions. Its broad lawns had been brutally torn up to accommodate trucks, piles of lumber, and a temporary construction shed. As the police car maneuvered around these obstacles, carpenters and electricians swarming over the site waved friendly salutes in the chief's direction. Brodie was a popular lawman, an amiable Scot with a towering figure, a beefy chest, and sturdy legs that looked appropriate with the kilt, tam-o'-shanter, and bagpipe that he brought out for parades and weddings.

As Brodie climbed the stairs to the apartment, Qwilleran greeted him from the top of the flight.

The chief was grumbling. He was always complaining about something. "They made the stairs too steep and too small when this place was built. There isn't room for a healthy man's foot."

"Walk up sideways," Qwilleran suggested.

"What's that thing?" Brodie pointed to a circle of ornamental wrought iron, a yard in diameter, leaning against the wall at the head of the stairs. Centered in the design were three cats rampant —scrappy animals—rearing on hind legs, ready to attack.

"That's from the gate of a three hundred-year-old Scottish castle." Qwilleran spoke with pride. "It's adapted from the Mackintosh coat of arms. My mother was a Mackintosh."

"Where'd you get it?" Brodie's envious manner indicated he would give anything for a similar memento of his own clan—or anything within reason; he was a thrifty man.

"From an antique shop Down Below. I left it in the city when I moved up to Pickax. Had it shipped up here last week."

"Looks heavy. Must've cost plenty for freight."

"It weighs about a hundred pounds. I'd like to incorporate it in my living room, but I don't know how."

"Ask my daughter. She has a lot of far-out ideas."

"Is that a commercial?" Qwilleran asked. Francesca Brodie was an interior designer.

With a bagpiper's swagger Brodie walked into the living room, giving it a policeman's quick once-over before flopping into a man-sized lounge chair. "You've got a comfortable roost here."

"Francesca's been helping me fix it up. When I lived in the mansion up front, this was an escape from too much opulence, but when I started living here full-time it suddenly looked bleak. How do you like what she put on the walls? Hand-woven Scottish tweed."

The chief turned to appraise the oatmeal-colored, oatmeal-textured wallcovering. "You shelled out plenty for that stuff, I bet. But I guess you can afford it." He then stared at the end wall. "You've got a lot of shelves."

"Francesca designed the shelf setup and had her carpenter build it. I'm starting to collect old books."

"With your bankroll you ought to be buying new books."

"I like old books. I bought a whole set of Dickens for ten bucks. You're a thrifty Scot; you should appreciate that."

"What's that picture?" Brodie pointed to a framed print over the sofa.

"An 1805 gunboat that used to sail the Great Lakes ... How about a free cup of coffee?" Qwilleran stirred heaping spoonfuls of instant coffee into boiling water and handed a mug to Brodie. "Okay, what's the bad news, chief? What's so urgent that you have to get me out of bed?"

"Just got back from a law-enforcement conference Down Below," Brodie said. "Glad to be back where life is civilized. I tell you, those cities down there are jungles. They stole the mayor's car the first day of the conference." He took a swallow of coffee and choked. "Och! This is rugged stuff!"

"What was the conference about?"

"Drug-related violence. One of the speakers was a friend of yours. Lieutenant Hames. I talked to him at lunch."

"Hames is a brilliant detective, although he likes to play dumb."

"He told me some things about you, too. He said you gave him some good tips when you were writing for the *Daily Fluxion*."

Qwilleran smoothed his moustache modestly. "Well, you know how it is. Things happen on a newspaper beat. I kept my eyes peeled and my ears flapping, that's all."

"Hames told me something else, too, and I thought he was putting me on, but he swears it's true. He says you have a very unusual cat. Very smart animal."

"He's right about that. Siamese are remarkably intelligent."

Brodie eyed his host keenly. "He says your cat is, like they say . . . psychic!"

"Wait a minute now. I wouldn't go that far, Brodie."

"He said your cat led the police to evidence that solved a couple of cases."

Qwilleran cleared his throat as he did before making a formal declamation. "You're a dog man, Brodie, so maybe you don't know this, but cats are the detectives of the animal world. They're naturally inquisitive. They're always sniffing around, scratching here and there, finding small places to sneak into, digging things out of holes. If my cat unearthed any clues, it was purely accidental."

"What's its name? I'd like to have a look at this cat."

"Koko is a seal-point Siamese, a neutered male, highly pedigreed. And don't call him 'it' or he'll put the whammy on you."

An imperious demand sounded from somewhere down the hall.

"That's Koko," Qwilleran said. "He heard his name mentioned, and he hasn't had his breakfast yet. I'll let him out. The cats have their own apartment."

"They do? I'll be damned!"

"With private bath and television."

"Television! You've gotta be kidding."

"Just a small black-and-white set. Cats don't see colors."

Enjoying Brodie's shock, Qwilleran excused himself and walked down the hall. The former servants' quarters over the garage provided him with a living room, writing studio, and bedroom. The fourth room—the one with the sunniest exposure—was reserved for the Siamese. It was furnished with soft carpet, cushions, baskets, scratching posts, and wide window sills facing south and west. In the bathroom were two commodes—his and hers. Originally they shared the same litter pan, but the female had developed a temperamental behavior pattern in recent weeks; she wanted her own facilities.

Qwilleran returned to the living room, followed by his two housemates, their body language demanding food. Two lean, fawn-colored bodies stretched to their longest; two brown masks with brown ears followed two brown noses uplifted in anticipation; two brown tails extended horizontally with a slight upcurve at the tip. They had the same kind of long, slender brown legs, but Koko walked with a resolute step while Yum Yum minced along daintily, a few paces behind him. At the living room entrance both animals stopped as if on cue and surveyed the stranger.

"They have blue eyes!" Brodie said. "I didn't know you had two. Are they from the same litter?"

"No, I adopted them from different sources," Qwilleran said. "Each one was left homeless under circumstances that Lieutenant Hames would probably remember."

The larger of the two sauntered into the room with a matter-of-fact gait and examined the visitor from a civil distance.

Qwilleran made the introductions. "Chief, this is Koko, the inspector general. He insists on screening everyone for security reasons. Koko, this is Chief Brodie of the Pickax police department."

The police chief and the cat stared at each other, the lawman with a puzzled frown. Then Koko leaped lightly to a bookshelf six feet off the floor.

Squeezing between Benjamin Franklin's *Autobiography* and Boswell's *Life of Johnson,* he settled down to monitor the newcomer from an aerial vantage point.

Brodie said, "He looks like an ordinary cat! I mean, you can tell he's purebred and all that, but . . ."

"Did you expect him to have green fur and electronic eyes and rotating antennae? I told you, Brodie, he's just a pet who happens to be normally inquisitive and unusually intelligent."

Brodie relaxed and turned his attention to the smaller Siamese, who was slowly approaching with graceful, pigeon-toed steps, all the while concentrating on his shoes.

"Meet Yum Yum the Paw," Qwilleran said. "She looks fragile, but she has a lightning-fast paw like a steel hook. She opens doors, unties shoelaces, and steals anything small and shiny. Watch out for your badge."

"We used to have cats on the farm," Brodie said, "but they never came indoors."

"These never go outdoors."

"Then how do they find anything to eat? You don't buy that expensive stuff in *little cans,* do you?"

"To tell the truth, Brodie, Koko refuses to eat anything labeled 'catfood.' He wants his meals freshly cooked."

The chief shook his head in disbelief or disapproval. "Hames told me you spoiled your cat rotten, and I guess he wasn't just beating his gums."

"Did you learn anything about drug-related violence at the conference?"

"Like I told Hames, drugs and violence aren't our problem up here. He didn't believe me."

"Neither do I, although I've heard you say it before."

"Sure, we've pulled up some funny plants in a couple of backyards, and a few years back the kids were sniffing this here airplane glue, but we don't have drug rings or drug pushers. Not yet, anyway."

"How do you account for it?"

"We're isolated—400 miles north of everywhere, like it says on the sign at city limits. Crackpot ideas are slow in reaching us. Hell, the fast-food chains haven't even discovered Moose County yet." Brodie took another swallow of coffee with a grim expression. "Another thing: we have good family life up here. We have a lot of church activities and organized sports and healthy outdoor hobbies like camping and hunting and fishing. It's a good place to bring up kids."

"If drugs and violence aren't the problem, what do you do to keep so busy? Write parking tickets?"

The chief scowled at him. "Drunk drivers! Underage drinking! Vandalism! That's what runs us ragged. When my girls were in high school, them and my wife and I were always going to funerals— you know, the funerals of their classmates—kids

getting themselves killed in car accidents. They'd be
driving fast, horsing around in a moving vehicle,
drinking beer illegally, hitting a patch of loose
gravel, losing control. But now we've got another
headache: vandalism in on the increase."

"I noticed that someone made power turns on the
courthouse lawn last week."

"That's what I mean. There's a certain element—a
few crazies—that don't have anything to do. They
shot out two streetlights on Goodwinter Boulevard
last night. When I was a kid we smashed pumpkins
and strung trees with toilet paper on Halloween, but
this new generation does it all year round. They pull
up the flowers in front of city hall. They bash rural
mailboxes with baseball bats. I don't understand
it!"

"I haven't seen any graffiti."

"Not yet, but they poured a can of paint on the
fountain in the park. We know the punks that are
doing it, but we never catch 'em in the act." Brodie
paused. He was looking hopefully at Qwilleran.

"Do you have a plan?"

"Well . . . after talking to Hames . . . I wondered
if your cat . . . could tip us off to where they're going to strike next, so we could stake it out."

Qwilleran eyed him askance. "What were you
guys smoking at that conference?"

"All I know is what Hames told me. He said your
cat has ESP or something."

"Listen, Brodie. Suppose that little animal who

is sitting on the bookshelf licking his tail—suppose he knew that vandals were going to heave a brick through the school window on June second at 2:45 A.M. Just how would he communicate this information? You're nuts, Brodie. I admit that Koko occasionally senses danger, but what you're suggesting is preposterous!"

"Out in California they're using cats to predict earthquakes."

"That's a whole different ballgame . . . How about more coffee? Your cup's empty."

"If I drank another cup of this battery acid, I'd be paralyzed from the neck down."

"After the suggestion you just made, I think you're paralyzed from the neck up. Who's the leader of this gang of hoodlums? Isn't there usually a leader? How old is he?"

"Nineteen and just out of high school. He comes from a good family, but he runs with a pack from Chipmunk. That's the slummiest town in the county, I guess you know. They get a few cans of beer and go cruising in their broken-down crates."

"What's his name?"

Brodie seemed reluctant to reveal it. "Well, I'm sorry to say . . . it's Chad Lanspeak."

"Not the department-store heir! Not the son of Carol and Larry!"

The chief nodded regretfully. "He's been in trouble ever since junior high."

"That's really bad news! His parents are just

about the finest people in town! Community leaders! Their older son is studying for the ministry, and their daughter is premed!"

"You're not telling me anything I don't know. Lanspeak is a good name. It's hard to figure out how Chad got off the track. People say the third child is always an oddball, and it may be true. Take my three girls, for instance. The two older ones got married right after school and started families. I've got four grandkids, and I'm not fifty yet. But Francesca! She was the third. She was determined to go away to college and have a career."

"But she returned to Pickax to work. You haven't lost her."

"Yes, she's a good girl, and she still lives at home. That's something we're thankful for. The family is still together. But she's all wrapped up in decorating and acting in plays."

"She has talent, Brodie. She's directing the next play at the Theatre Club. You should be proud of her."

"That's what my wife says."

"Francesca is twenty-four, and she has to make her own choices."

The police chief seemed unconvinced. "She could have married into the Fitch family. She dated David Fitch when they were in high school. That's another fine old family. David's great-grandfather struck it rich in the 1880s—in mining or lumbering, I forget which. David and Harley went to Yale, and now they're vice presidents at the bank. Their dad is bank president. Fine man, Nigel Fitch! I thought sure I was going to have one of the boys for a son-in-law."

Brodie looked away sadly. His disappointment was painful to witness.

"One of my daughters married a farmer," he went on, "and the other one married an electrician with his own business. Decent fellas, they are. Ambitious. Good providers. But Francesca could have married David Fitch. She used to bring him and Harley home after school to listen to that noise the kids call music. They were real gentlemen. 'Hello, Mr. Brodie' and 'How are you, Mr. Brodie?' They liked to hear me play the pipes. Nice boys. Nothing snobbish about them at all. Full of fun, too."

"They're fine young men," Qwilleran agreed. "I've met them at the Theatre Club."

"Talk about talent! They're in all the plays. They were the twins in a musical called "The Boys from Poughkeepsie" or something like that. Nigel is lucky to have sons like those two. Francesca really passed up a good chance."

"Yow!" said Koko in a sudden irritable commentary on the conversation, as if he were bored.

"Well, to get back to my suggestion," Brodie said. "Give it a thought or two. I'd like to break up this gang before they get into something worse, like torching barns or breaking into summer cottages or stealing cars. That can happen, you know."

"Did you ever talk to Carol and Larry about their son?"

The chief threw up his hands. "Many times. They keep up a brave front, but they're heartbroken. What parent wouldn't be? The boy doesn't live at home. He drifts around, shacking up wherever he can, partying all night. Never wanted to go to college."

"What does he do for money?"

"As I understand it, his grandmother left him a trust fund, but he doesn't get his monthly check unless he goes to college or works in the family store—Larry put him in charge of sporting goods—but he goofs off half the time and goes hunting or trapping. Poaching, most likely."

"I feel bad about this," Qwilleran said. "The Lanspeaks don't deserve this kind of trouble."

"You know, Qwill, you bachelors are lucky. You don't have any problems."

"Don't be too sure."

"What's your problem?"

"Women."

"What did I tell you!" Brodie said in triumph. "I told you they'd all be chasing after you. A fella can't inherit millions like you did and expect to live a normal life. If you don't mind some advice, I say you should get yourself a wife and get your name off the eligible list."

"I had a wife," Qwilleran said. "It didn't work out."

"So try it again! Marry a young woman and start thinking about heirs. You're not too old for that."

"When I go, I'm leaving everything to the Klingenschoen Memorial Fund. They'll distribute it right here in Moose County, where the money was made and where it belongs."

"I suppose all kinds of people are bugging you for handouts."

"The Fund takes care of that, too. I turn everything over to them. They dole it out to charities and good causes and give me a little to live on."

"Och! You're a little daft. Did anybody ever tell you?"

"I've never wanted a lot of money or possessions."

"I noticed that," said Brodie, glancing around the room. "How many millionaires or billionaires live over the garage? Did you ever see how the Fitches live? Nigel and his wife have a double condominium at Indian Village, and Francesca says it's really fixed up! Harley and his bride have the old Fitch mansion that looks like a castle. Twenty-two rooms! David and Jill have a new house that's going to be on the cover of some magazine . . . I tell you, Qwill, Fran really blew it when she didn't marry David Fitch. But it's too late now."

After Brodie had made his departure, maneuvering down the stairs and complaining about the narrow treads, Qwilleran mixed another cup of instant coffee in the four-by-four-foot closet that served as his kitchen. He also warmed up some two-day-old doughnuts in the miniature microwave.

Koko jumped down from the biography shelf and started prowling like a caged tiger, yikking and yowling because his breakfast was late. Yum Yum sat hunched up in a bundle of self-pity for the same reason.

"Cool it," Qwilleran told Koko, after consulting his watch. "The chuckwagon will be here any minute."

When he and the Siamese lived up front in the mansion, they had a housekeeper who spoiled all three of them with home-cooked delicacies. Now Qwilleran took lunch and dinner in restaurants, and the cats' meals were catered by the chef at the Old Stone Mill. A busboy named Derek Cuttlebrink made daily deliveries of poultry, meat, and seafood that needed only to be warmed with a little of the accompanying sauce.

When Derek finally arrived with the shrimp timbales in lobster puree, he apologized for being late and said, "The chef wants to know how they liked the veal blanquette yesterday."

"Okay, except for the Japanese mushrooms, Derek. They don't like Japanese mushrooms. And tell him not to send marinated artichoke hearts— only the fresh ones. Their favorite food is turkey, but it must be off-the-bird—not that rolled stuff."

He tipped the busboy and sat down to finish his

coffee and watch the Siamese devouring their food. Each cat was a study in concentration—tail flat on the floor, whiskers swept back out of the way. Then they washed up fastidiously, and Yum Yum leaped into Qwilleran's lap, landing as softly as a cloud and turning around three times before settling down. Koko arranged himself on the biography shelf and waited for the dialogue to begin.

Qwilleran made it a policy to converse with the cats; it seemed more rational than talking to himself, as he had a tendency to do after living alone so long. Koko in particular seemed to enjoy the sound of a human voice. He responded as if he understood every word.

"Well, Koko, what do you think of Brodie's ridiculous suggestion?"

"Yow," said the cat with an inflection that sounded like disdain.

"The poor guy's really disappointed that Fran didn't marry into the Fitch family. I wonder if he knows she's making a play for me."

"Nyik nyik," said Koko, shifting his position nervously. He had never been enthusiastic about any of the women in Qwilleran's life.

Qwilleran had first met Fran Brodie when he started buying furniture from Amanda's Studio of Interior Design. Amanda was middle-aged, gray-haired, dowdy, tactless and irascible, but he liked her. Her assistant was young, attractive and friendly, and he liked her also. Both women wore neutral col-

ors that would not compete with the fabrics and
wallpapers they showed to clients, but on Amanda
the beige, gray, khaki and taupe looked drab; on
Francesca's willowy figure they looked chic. More
and more Amanda retired into the background, running the business while her vivacious assistant
worked with the clients.

Fran was tall like her father, with the same gray
eyes and strawberry-blond hair, but her eyes had a
steely glint of ambition and determination.

"She knows I'm involved with Polly Duncan,"
Qwilleran said, "but it doesn't slow her down. Polly
warned me about joining the Theatre Club and hir-
ing Fran, but I thought it was just female catti-
ness . . ."

"YOW!" said Koko sternly.

"Sorry. I didn't mean that. Let's say it looked like
an older woman's jealousy of a young rival, and
Fran is really on the make! I don't know whether
she's after me or the Klingenschoen money."

"Nyik nyik," Koko said.

"The aggressiveness of the new generation is hard
for me to accept. I may be old-fashioned, but I like
to do the chasing."

Francesca's strategy was all too transparent. She
had asked for a key to his apartment, in order, she
said, to supervise the workmen and the delivery of
merchandise. She brought wallpaper-sample books
and furniture catalogues for his perusal, entailing
consultations in close proximity on the sofa, with

pictures and patterns spread out on their laps and with knees accidentally touching. She timed these tête-à-têtes for the cocktail hour, when it was only polite for Qwilleran to offer a drink or two, after which a dinner invitation was almost obligatory. She suggested that they fly Down Below for a few days to select furniture and art objects at design centers and galleries. She wanted to do over his bedroom with draped walls, a fur bedcover, and mirrored ceiling.

Francesca was attractive without doubt. She bubbled with youthful vitality, wore enticing scents, and had legs that looked provocative with high-heeled sandals. Having turned fifty, however, Qwilleran was beginning to feel more comfortable with women of his own age who wore size 16. Polly Duncan was head librarian at the Pickax Public Library, and she shared his interest in literature as no other woman had ever done. Following the tragic death of her husband many years before, she was now rediscovering love, and her responses were warm and caring, belying her outward show of reserve. They were discreet about their relationship, but there were few secrets in Pickax, and everyone knew about the librarian and the Klingenschoen heir, and also about the interior designer.

"Polly is getting edgy," Qwilleran said to his attentive listener. "I don't like what jealousy does to a woman. She's intelligent and admirable in every way, and yet . . . the brainiest ones sometimes lose control. Sooner or later there's going to be an explosion! Do you think librarians ever commit crimes of passion?"

"Yow," said Koko as he scratched his ear with his hind foot.

SCENE TWO

Place: Downtown Pickax
Time: The following morning
Cast: HIXIE RICE, a young woman from
      Down Below
      EDDINGTON SMITH, dealer in used
      books
      CHAD, the black sheep of the
      Lanspeak family
      Construction workers, pedestrians,
      clerks

Qwilleran decided to take a casual walk downtown after hearing the 9 A.M. newscast on station

WPKX. "Vandals opened fire hydrants during the night, seriously draining the city's water supply and impeding firefighters called to a burning building on the west side."

As a veteran journalist who had written for major newspapers around the country, Qwilleran despised the headline news on the radio—those twenty-five-word teasers sandwiched between two hundred-word commercials. They only fueled the feud between the print and electronic media. He stormed around his apartment, ranting aloud—to the alarm of the Siamese.

"How many hydrants were opened? Where were they located? What was the extent of water loss? What was the cost to the city? Whose building burned as a result? When was the vandalism discovered? Why did no one notice the gushing water?"

The Siamese flew about the apartment as they always did when Qwilleran went on a rampage.

"Well, never mind. Excuse the outburst," he said in a calmer mood, tamping his moustache. "In a few days we'll get our news from print coverage."

Moose County had been without a good newspaper for several years, and now the situation was about to be corrected. Thanks to the Klingenschoen Memorial Fund and some prodding from Qwilleran, a paper of professional caliber would hit the streets on Wednesday next.

Meanwhile, there were only two adequate sources of news. One could plug into the grapevine that flourished in the coffee shops, on the courthouse steps, and over back fences. Or one could wander into the police station when the talkative Brodie was on duty.

"I'm going downtown to do a few errands," Qwilleran informed his housemates. "Mr. O'Dell will be coming in to clean, and he has orders not to give you any handouts, so don't put on your phony starvation act. See you later."

Koko and Yum Yum listened impassively and then accompanied him to the head of the stairs, where they both rubbed jaws against the Mackintosh coat of arms until their fangs clicked on the wrought iron. Qwilleran often wondered about their silent farewells. Were they sorry to see him go, or glad? Were they worried or relieved? Who could tell what was behind those mysterious blue eyes?

He always walked downtown. Everything in Pickax was within walking distance, although few of the locals ever used their legs for transportation. As he walked down the long driveway, the construction crew working on the renovation of the mansion greeted him jovially, and the job supervisor tossed him a hard hat and invited him into the building to inspect their progress.

The Klingenschoen mansion, three stories high and built of fieldstone two-feet thick, had been completely gutted in preparation for the conversion, and the interior was redesigned to provide amphitheater seating, a thrust stage, a professional lighting system, and adequate dressing rooms. It would seat three hundred and would be the new home of the Theatre Club.

"Will it be finished on schedule?" Qwilleran asked.

"Hopefully, if the architects don't give us any flak," said the supervisor. "Someone's flying up from Down Below to make an inspection next week. I hope they don't send that girl architect. She's a tough baby."

Qwilleran chuckled at the remark. The architectural firm was a Cincinnati outfit specializing in small theater design, and the "tough baby" was Alacoque Wright, a flighty young woman he had dated Down Below before she eloped with an engineer. He resumed his walk, marveling at the quirks of fate and anticipating a reunion with Cokey.

The three blocks of Main Street that constituted downtown Pickax were unique. In its heyday the town had been the hub of the mining and quarrying industry in the county, and all commercial buildings were constructed of stone. What made the cityscape unusual was the design of the stores and office buildings, which masqueraded as miniature castles, temples, fortresses and monasteries, reflecting the flamboyant taste of nineteenth-century mining tycoons.

Walking past the public library (housed in a Greek temple), Qwilleran automatically looked for Polly Duncan's cranberry-red car in the parking lot. In front of the lodge hall (a small-scale Bastille) a volunteer shaking a canister for the "Save Our

Snakes" fund flashed an irresistible smile, and he donated a dollar. As he passed Scottie's Men's Shop (a Cotswold cottage) a young woman breezed out of the store with her hair flying, her shoulder bag flying, and yards of skirt flying. It was Hixie Rice, the exuberant advertising manager of the new Moose County newspaper. She had been his neighbor Down Below, and he had been instrumental in bringing her to Pickax.

"Hi, Qwill!" she trilled.

"Morning, Hixie. How's it going?"

"Like you wouldn't *believe!* I sold Scottie a double spread for the opener, and he signed a twenty-six-week contract. Even that weird bookstore took a quarter page. And today I'm lunching at the country club with three bankers! Nigel Fitch is charming, and his sons are adorable, especially the one with a moustache. Too bad they're all married."

"I didn't know that made much difference to you."

"Forget my lurid past Down Below," she said with an airy gesture. "In Pickax I'm *totally* discreet. I've given up married men, cigarettes, and high heels. I bought seven pairs of skimmers at Lanspeak's, and I skim everywhere. What are you doing for dinner tonight? I'll buy."

"Sorry, Hixie, but I've got a date."

"Okay. Catch you later." She skimmed across Main Street in the middle of the block, dodging cars, vans, and pickups with deft footwork, throwing kisses to the drivers who whistled in appreciation or honked horns in annoyance.

Qwilleran headed for the bookstore that Hixie called weird. For once she had not exaggerated. It literally crouched on the backstreet behind Lanspeak's department store. Rough stones were piled up to simulate a grotto, and the stone was feldspar; on a sunny day it glittered like the front of a burlesque house. Hanging alongside the front door was a weathered sign, almost illegible: EDD'S EDITIONS. In the grimy front window were old books with drab covers, and one drooping potted plant.

The interior of the store was as dim as the feldspar exterior was dazzling. Coming in from the sunshine Qwilleran could see nothing at first, but he blinked until the scene took shape: tables loaded with haphazard piles of dingy books, floor-to-ceiling shelves jammed with grayish bindings and invisible titles, a shaky wooden stepladder, and a smoky-gray Persian cat walking across a table of old magazines, waving his plume of a tail like a feather duster. The place had a smell of old books and sardines.

Qwilleran's arrival had activated a tinkling bell on the front door, and soon the proprietor materialized from the shadows. Eddington Smith was a small, thin man with gray hair and a gray complexion and nondescript gray clothing. He reminded Qwilleran of someone else he had known, except for his bland smile—a permanent smile expressing utter contentment.

"Greetings," the man said, softly and pleasantly.

"Morning, Edd. Nice day, isn't it? How's Winston?" Qwilleran stroked the cat, and Winston accepted the attention with the dignity of a prime minister. "How old is this building, Edd? It's so hideous, it's fascinating."

"It's over a hundred years old—a blacksmith's shop originally. They say the mason who built it was strange in the head." He spoke gently and kindly.

"I believe it."

" 'We shape our buildings, thereafter they shape us,' to quote Mr. Churchill. I guess it's true. My grandfather said the blacksmith was a regular caveman."

"Apparently the building hasn't had the same effect on you," Qwilleran said genially.

"That's right," Eddington said, still smiling. "I feel like something that lives under a stone. Dr. Halifax says I spend too much time in the shop. He says I should get out and join a club and have some fun. I'm not sure I'd like fun."

"Dr. Hal is a wise man. You should take his advice."

" 'Work is much more fun than fun!' That's what Noel Coward said . . . Is there something I can do for you today? Or do you want to browse?"

"I'm interested in finding a set of Brittanica published in 1910."

"The eleventh edition!" The bookseller nodded in approval. "I'll see what I can do. I'm still searching for your Shakespeare."

"Remember, I want the plays in separate volumes. They're easier to read."

Eddington's smile looked roguish. "A British scholar called Shakespeare the sexiest writer in the English language."

"That's why he's been popular for four hundred years." Qwilleran gave Winston two more strokes and started for the door.

Eddington followed him. "You belong to the Theatre Club, don't you?"

"Yes, I joined recently. I'm being initiated with a role in the next play."

"Harley Fitch invited me to join. Do you know Harley? He's a nice young man. Very friendly."

Qwilleran edged closer to the door.

"I wouldn't be good at acting," said the bookseller, "but I could open and close the curtain, I suppose—something like that."

"Once you get up on that stage, Edd, you might discover hidden talents." Qwilleran now had his hand on the doorhandle.

"I don't think so. The others in the club are all smart and well-educated. Harley Fitch and his brother went to Yale. I've never been to college."

"You may not have a degree," Qwilleran assured him, "but you're a very well-read man."

Eddington lowered his head, smiling modestly, and Qwilleran took the opportunity to escape into the sunshine. He wondered about the enigmatic little man. How did he stay in business? How did he earn enough to buy sardines for Winston? There were never any customers in the store. He sold no greeting cards or paper napkins or scented candles as a sideline. Just old, faded, dusty, musty books.

Qwilleran also gave some thought to the celebrated Fitch family, a name that everyone mentioned with respect, if not adoration. The Fitches were "friendly . . . charming . . . clean-cut . . . a fine old family . . . real gentlemen . . . fun-loving . . . clever." The adulation could become cloying.

He stopped for a cup of coffee at the luncheonette and then went to the police station, where he found Brodie on the sergeant's desk. "The kids went cruising again last night," he said to the chief.

"Och! It's no laughing matter," Brodie said. "It'll cost the city a few hundred in water revenue, and a family on the west side saw their house burn down to the ground for lack of water pressure."

"How many hydrants did the vandals open?"

"Eight. They used pipe wrenches, so there's no damage to the hydrants themselves. I suppose we should be grateful to the delinquents for being so considerate."

"Where were the hydrants located?"

"East Township Line—industrial area—deserted at night. It happened about three or four in the morning, judging by the amount of water wasted. Senseless! Senseless!"

"When was it discovered?"

"About six o'clock this morning. The low pressure set off a sprinkler alarm at the plastics factory, and that alerted the fire department. Right after that the call came in from the west side."

"Whose house burned down?"

"Young couple with three kids and no insurance. There wasn't enough water in the tank to put the fire down. Mind you, two hundred and fifty thousand gallons lost! What gets me is this—we have plenty of floods and forest fires and tornadoes and hurricanes and droughts. We don't need man-made disasters as well."

"How come the prowl car didn't spot the gushing water during the night?"

Brodie leaned back in his chair wearily. "Listen. We have a force of six men, including me and the sergeant. There are seven days in the week and twenty-four hours in the day—and all this damned paperwork! That spreads us pretty thin. On Friday nights we have two cars out on the beat. That's payday, you know; the boozers whoop it up and sleep it off on Saturday. So we concentrate on the bars and party stores and school parking lot. There was a big dance at the school last night, and after that the kids went partying in the neighborhoods— making noise, raising hell, all the usual. We logged I don't know how many DPs. There were two brawls at taverns and three car accidents, and that's just within the city limits! Drivers and passengers all sloshed! Then there was a minor fire in a foster home for the elderly—some old geezer smoking in bed. No damage, but enough panic for a major earthquake! I tell you, Qwill, Friday night is hell-night in Pickax, especially in spring—just like it was a hundred years ago when the lumberjacks used to come into town and mix it up with the miners."

"I can see you had your hands full," Qwilleran said. "What were the state troopers doing all this time?"

"Oh, they assisted—when they weren't chasing drunk drivers all over the county. One high-speed chase ended up with the guy in the Ittibittiwassee River."

"It looks as if the vandalism is escalating, as you predicted."

"When they get tired of pulling up flowers, they look for bigger kicks. This is Saturday. They'll be out again tonight." Brodie looked at Qwilleran inquiringly. "There should be some way to outguess them."

"Forget about cat power, Brodie. It won't work." Qwilleran saluted the chief and went on his way. He wanted to make one more stop before lunch. He wanted to meet the black sheep of the Lanspeak family.

The department store was the largest commercial building on Main Street—a Byzantine palace with banners flying from the battlements. That was the kind of dramatic touch that would appeal to Larry Lanspeak. He and his wife, Carol, were the lifeblood of the Theatre Club. Their energy and enthusiasm were legendary in Pickax; so was their store. In the 1880s it had served Moose County as a small general store, selling kerosene, gun powder, harnesses, crackers, cheese, and calico by the yard. Now the inventory included perfume and satin chemises, microwave ovens and television sets, fishing rods, and sweat shirts.

Sweat shirts! That was Qwilleran's cue. He headed for the men's casual wear in the rear of the store. It meant zigzagging through the women's department with their seductive aromas and silky displays. Clerks who had sold him sweaters, robes, and blouses in Polly Duncan's size brightened when they saw him.

"Morning, Mr. Q."

"Help you, Mr. Q? We just received some lovely silk scarfs. Real silk!"

In the sporting goods department a young man was leaning on a glass showcase, poring over a gun catalogue. His pigtail and Fu-Manchu moustache looked ludicrous for a conservative town like Pickax.

"Do you have any sweat shirts?" Qwilleran asked him.

"On the rack." The clerk jerked his head toward the casual wear with a look of boredom.

"Do you have any in green?"

"What's on the rack, that's what we've got."

"How much are they?"

"Different prices. Whatever it says on the tag."

"I'm sorry, but I didn't bring my reading glasses," Qwilleran said. "Would you be good enough to help me?" It was a lie, but he enjoyed irritating clerks who irritated him.

Reluctantly the young man left his gun catalogue and found a green sweat shirt in a large size and at a price that seemed fair. While the sale was being written up, Qwilleran looked at fishing rods and reels, bows and arrows, hunting knives, lifebelts, backpacks, and other gear that had nothing to do with his lifestyle. He spotted one item, however, that would be most inconvenient for a lazy clerk to reach: a pair of snowshoes hung high on the wall.

"Are those the only snowshoes you have?" he inquired.

"We don't stock snowshoes in spring."

"What are they made of?"

"Aluminum."

"I'd like to examine them."

"I'll have to get a ladder."

"That sounds like a good idea," Qwilleran said, enjoying his script and performance.

After some exertion and disgruntled muttering the young man brought down the snowshoes, and Qwilleran studied them leisurely.

"How do you keep them on your feet?"

"Bindings."

"Which is the back and which is the front?"

"The tail is the back."

"That makes sense," Qwilleran said. "Is this the only kind you ever carry?"

"In winter we have some with wood frames and cowhide lacing."

"Do you do any snowshoeing yourself?"

"When I check my traps."

"Do you use aluminum or wood?"

"Wood, but I make my own."

"You make your own snowshoes? How do you do that?" There was a note of sincere amazement in the question.

The clerk showed some slight signs of life. "Cut down a white ash to make the frames. Kill a deer to get the hide for lacing."

"Incredible! How did you learn to do it?"

The fellow shrugged and looked half-pleased. "Just found out, that's all."

"How do you make a curved frame out of a tree?"

"Cut it to the right size, steam it and bend it, that's all."

"Amazing! I'm new in the north country," Qwilleran said, "but snowshoeing is something I'd like to try next winter. Is it hard to do?"

"Just put one foot in front of the other. And don't be in a hurry."

"How fast do you go?"

"Depends on the snow—hardpack or soft—and whether you're in underbrush. Four miles an hour is pretty fast."

"Do they come in different sizes?"

"Different sizes and different styles. I've made all kinds—Michigan, Bear Paw, arctic—all kinds."

"Do you make them to sell?"

"Never did, but . . ."

"I'd like to buy a handmade pair, if I could see a selection."

member, you think you're Teddy Roosevelt charging up San Juan Hill."

"You don't know what you're asking, Fran. I'm laid-back by choice and by temperament, and getting more so every year."

"Make an adjustment," she said with the sweet smile she always employed to get what she wanted. "You'll be able to practice with the bugle tomorrow night if Harley remembers to bring it."

Qwilleran said, "The Fitch twins are the ones who'll steal the show—Harley in his Boris Karloff makeup, and David playing that slimy doctor like a perfect creep."

"They're two talented boys," Fran said, "and such good sports. They're really wasted on banking." She glanced at her watch, yet seemed in no hurry to leave.

"I'm glad you gave Eddington a part to play, even though he's terrified."

"He'll be perfect for old Mr. Gibbs, won't he? But I hope he learns to project. He speaks in a whisper."

"No one ever shouts in a bookstore, and that's where he's spent his whole life."

"Anyway, here's what I wanted to discuss, Qwill. We want to do *Bell, Book and Candle* for our summer show, and we'll need a cat to play Pyewacket. Do you think . . ."

"No, I don't think Koko would care for the role. He's extremely independent. He doesn't take direction. And he prefers his own script."

"Maybe we should announce a public audition and invite people to bring their cats."

"You'd have a riot!" Qwilleran said. "You'd have three hundred cat lovers with three hundred cats, all wailing and spitting and fighting and climbing up the curtain. And the humans would be even worse—pushy, indignant, belligerent. A company tried it Down Below, and they had to call the police."

"But it would generate publicity. When the newspaper starts publishing, we'll get all kinds of coverage. They've promised to review our productions."

"They're dreaming! Who'll qualify as a drama critic in Moose County?"

"You," she said with her sweet smile.

Qwilleran huffed into his moustache. "How can I sit in the fifth row, center, taking notes at the same time I'm onstage blowing the bugle and charging up San Juan Hill?"

"You'll figure it out." She could be infuriatingly illogical one minute and a frighteningly straight thinker the next. "Will the theater be ready on schedule?"

"They've promised, but anything can happen in the building trades: electricians are electrocuted; plumbers drown; painters inhale toxic fumes; carpenters bleed to death."

"What would you think of an original revue for the grand opening, instead of a Broadway play?"

"What kind of material?"

"Humorous skits . . . witty parodies . . . a chorus line . . . comic acts. Harley and David have a funny twin act that they do. Susan danced in college; she can do choreography."

"Do you have a theme in mind?"

"It should be a spoof of contemporary life, don't you think? I mean—politics, television, fashion, pop music, the IRS—anything. Preferably tied in with Moose County."

"And who would write these humorous skits and witty parodies?" he demanded.

"You!" There was that tantalizing smile again.

Qwilleran growled a protest. "That would take a lot of time and thought, and you know I'm writing a novel, Fran."

She looked at her watch. "Well, think about it. Now I've got to go home. I'm expecting a long-distance call from Mother. She's visiting my aunt Down Below. Thanks for your input, Qwill. See you tomorrow night at seven sharp."

Qwilleran walked home slowly, enjoying the soft breezes of a spring evening. On Monday nights the downtown area was always deserted, and an eerie silence fell upon Main Street. His footsteps echoed in the canyon created by the stone buildings.

The idea of an original revue began to appeal to him. He had written student shows in college. It might be fun to write parodies of well-known songs, one for each town in Moose County. The early settlers had given them outlandish names: Sawdust City, Chipmunk, Squunk Corners, Middle Hummock, West Middle Hummock, Wildcat, Smith's

Folly, Mooseville, even a village named Brrr. (It was the coldest spot in the county.)

The parodies would be easy, he thought. He tried a few opening lines, and his rich baritone reverberated in the stone canyon:

"Everything's out of date in Sawdust City . . ."
"Way down upon the Ittibittiwassee . . ."
"Mid-dle Hum-mock, here I come! . . ."
"April in Chipmunk; ragweed in blossom . . ."
"When it's Big Mosquito time in Mooseville . . ."
"I'm just wild about Wildcat . . ."

All too soon he reached the Park Circle. Here Main Street divided and circled a small park, on the perimeter of which were two churches, the courthouse, the public library, and the future theater. There was a nightlight in the construction shed, but the long driveway to the carriage house was in darkness. The moon had ducked behind a cloud, and he had forgotten to turn on the exterior lights at the corners of the carriage house.

He unlocked the door leading to the upstairs apartment and reached inside to flick the wall switch. The light fixture did not respond; neither did the light at the top of the stairs. A power outage, he supposed. The local joke was that Pickax blacked out if the weatherman even predicted a thunder storm. He started to mount the stairs in the dark. Brodie was right; they were steep, and the treads were narrow. They seemed narrower and steeper in total darkness. Slowly and carefully he went up, gripping the handrail.

Halfway to the top Qwilleran stopped. There was a strong odor in the stairwell—almost like coffee—or something burning. Electrical wires? He had a fear of fire when the cats were home alone.

At that moment he heard a sound he could not identify. He listened hard. The cats were locked in their apartment at the far end of the building, and it was not an animal sound; it was a scraping, like metal on wood. He remembered the wrought-iron coat of arms leaning against the wall in the upper hallway. If it came crashing down the stairs, it would send him flying to the bottom of the flight. He flattened himself against the wall and slid upward, one cautious step at a time.

In the upper hall he paused and listened. He felt a presence. There was no sound, but someone was there—breathing. The living-room door was open, and he was sure he had closed it before leaving. The total darkness indicated that the blinds were closed, and he was sure he had left them open. Now he was positive he could hear breathing, and he saw two red eyes glowing in the blacked-out room.

Stealthily he groped for the light switch inside the door, hoping it was operative. His hand touched something hairy.

From his throat came a horrendous roar—like a trapped lion, a wounded elephant, and a sick camel. It was a curse he had learned in North Africa.

Instantly there was light, and a chorus of tremulous voices managed a weak "Happy birthday!"

There were two dozen persons in the room, looking either shaken or sheepish or guilty.

"Dammit, you knuckleheads!" Qwilleran bellowed. "You could give a guy a heart attack! . . . What's this?"

Towering above him was a black bear with glass eyes and gaping jaws, rearing on hind legs, one paw over the light switch.

The two glowing spots of red were lights on a small machine. It stood on the travertine card table, plugged in and bubbling.

"I'm sorry," said Francesca. "It was my idea. We used the key you gave me."

Harley Fitch said, "My clone gets credit for the dramatic staging."

"My clone unscrewed the lightbulbs," said his brother, David, the one with a moustache. "He stood on my shoulders and ruined my golf swing permanently."

Qwilleran confronted Francesca. "So that's why you kept me overtime. I wondered why you looked at your watch every five minutes."

Larry Lanspeak said, "We needed a half hour to get set up. We had to park our cars out of sight and hike over here and wrestle the bear up those damn stairs and then hide Wally's van."

Wally Toddwhistle, a young taxidermist, said, "I happened to have the bear in my van. I'm delivering it to a customer."

"How did you guys know it's my birthday?"

Fran said, "Dad ran a check on your driver's registration."

"And what's that thing?" He pointed to the machine with the two red lights.

"That's a gift from all of us," said David's wife. "A protest against the lethal coffee you serve. You set it for the number of cups you want and the strength you prefer. A timer turns it on."

Then someone produced paper plates and cups, and someone else unveiled a sheet cake decorated with a bugle and the theater's traditional wish: "Break a leg, darling!"

As Qwilleran began to simmer down, the cast and crew of *Arsenic and Old Lace* relaxed. They were all there: Carol Lanspeak and Susan Exbridge, who were playing the wacky old sisters; Larry Lanspeak, a versatile character actor; Harley and David Fitch, who liked to do drunks, weirdos, and monsters; David's clever wife, Jill, who designed sets and costumes; Wally Toddwhistle, a genius at building sets out of orange crates, baling wire, and glue; Derek Cuttlebrink, who was attempting his first role; Eddington Smith, painfully ill at ease; and other members of the troupe whom Qwilleran knew only slightly. They were all talking at once:

Susan: "Darling, your entrance in the second act was marvelous!"

Fran: "An integrated actor thinks with his whole body, Derek."

Carol: "How's your wife, Harley?"

Harley: "Okay, but kind of grouchy. The doctor told her to quit smoking till after the baby comes."

Wally: "What's that big round iron thing in the hallway?"

Qwilleran: "It came from a castle in Scotland. Part of a gate, I think."

Larry: "At every performance she went up, and I had to ad-lib the whole scene. I could have killed her!"

David: "I grew a moustache to play the villain in *The Drunkard* because I'm allergic to spirit gum, and then I decided to keep it. Jill likes it."

Derek: "Where are the cats?"

Qwilleran: "In their apartment, watching the tube. Shall I let them out?"

Koko and Yum Yum made their entrance walking shoulder to shoulder like a team of horses. In the doorway they stopped abruptly, their ears, whiskers, noses, and blue eyes sensing the situation: noisy strangers, eating and dropping crumbs. In the next instant they sensed the black bear looming above them. Yum Yum bushed her tail, humped her back, sleeked her ears and whiskers, slanted her eyes, and made a wicked display of fangs. Koko crept cautiously toward the beast with his belly dragging the floor until convinced that it was harmless. Then he bravely sniffed its hind legs and rose up to paw the stiff-haired pelt. Next he turned his attention to the taxidermist, who was nervously guarding his handiwork. Koko subjected Wally Toddwhistle to a thorough inspection with his wet nose.

"He knows you work with animals," Qwilleran explained, by way of excusing Koko's impolite nuzzling.

Wally was flattered, however. "If a cat likes you," he said earnestly, "it means you have a princely character. That's what my mother always says."

Harley Fitch raised his right hand in affirmation. "If Wally's mother says so, it's gospel truth, believe me!"

"Amen," said David.

"Who's buying the bear?" Qwilleran asked the young taxidermist.

"Gary Pratt—for his bar at the Hotel Booze. I have to deliver it tonight when I leave here. Do you know Gary? My mother says he looks more like a bear than the bear does."

"Hear! Hear!" said Harley.

Next, Koko discovered that some of the noisy strangers were sitting on the floor, which was his domain by divine right. He stalked them and scolded, "Nyik nyik nyik!"

Meanwhile, Yum Yum had calmed down and was checking out sandals, western boots, and double-tied running shoes, none of which interested her. Then she discovered Eddington Smith's laced oxfords. The bookseller stood shyly apart from the others, and Qwilleran went over to speak to him.

Eddington said, "I've found some Shakespeare

comedies for you. An old lady in Squunk Corners had them in her attic. They're in good condition." He spoke softly, smiled blandly.

"I didn't know . . . the Bard had a following . . . in Squunk Corners," Qwilleran said absently as he kept an eye on the cats. Yum Yum was gleefully untying the man's shoelaces. Koko was exploring his socks and trouser legs with intent nose, forward whiskers, and a wild gleam in his eye.

"People up here," Eddington explained, "used to collect rare books, fine bindings, and first editions. Rich people, I mean. It was the thing to do."

"When the newspaper starts publishing they ought to send a reporter to your shop to get an interview."

"I don't think I'd be very good for an interview," said the bookseller. "I bought an ad, though—just a quarter page. I never advertised before, but a nice young lady came in and told me I should." Guiltily he added, " 'Advertising is . . . a campaign of subversion against intellectual honesty and moral integrity.' Somebody said that. I think it was Toynbee."

"Your character won't be compromised by a quarter page," Qwilleran assured him.

At that moment Harley Fitch walked up with the cake tray, and Koko transferred his attention to the bank vice president, rubbing his ankles, nipping his jeans, and purring hoarsely.

"Have some cake, Edd," said Harley in his heartiest voice, as if the bookseller were deaf.

"I've had two pieces already. 'Reason should direct and appetite obey.'"

"Who said that, Edd?"

"Cicero."

"Cicero would want you to have another piece of cake. How often do you go to a birthday party?"

Wistfully Eddington said, "I've never been to a birthday party before."

"Not even your own?"

The little man shook his head and smiled his bland all-purpose smile.

"Okay! For your birthday we'll have a party on the stage of the new theater, with a ten-foot sheet cake. You can blow out the candles before an audience of three hundred."

Pleasure fought with disbelief in the bookseller's gray face.

"We'll have it proclaimed Eddington Smith Day in Pickax."

David, hearing the commotion, joined the act. "We'll have a parade with floats and the high-school band, and fireworks in the evening."

Jill Fitch drew Qwilleran aside. "Aren't they crazy?" she said. "But they'll do it! They'll have the parade, the fireworks, and a proclamation from the mayor—or even the governor. That's the way they are." She lowered her voice. "Want to come to a surprise housewarming for Harley and Belle on Saturday night? They've moved into the old Fitch mansion, you know. Bring your own bottle."

"How about a gift?"

"No gifts. God knows they don't need anything. Have you seen Grandpa Fitch's house? It's loaded with stuff. I don't know how Harley can live with all those mounted animals and marble nymphs."

"I've never met Belle," Qwilleran said. "Doesn't she ever come to rehearsals?"

Jill shrugged. "She doesn't feel comfortable with this crowd. I guess we come on a little strong. And now that she's pregnant, Harley says she feels self-conscious."

It was a noisy party, with twenty-four club members crowded into a room designed for one man and two cats. Carol Lanspeak laughed a lot. Larry did impersonations of his more eccentric customers. Susan Exbridge, a fortyish divorcée, invited Qwilleran to a dance at the country club, but he pleaded another engagement; she served on the library board, and he feared Polly would hear about it. Eddington Smith said he'd never had such a good time in his life. Harley Fitch was flattered by Koko's advances and asked if he could take him home.

After the crowd had departed, Qwilleran made another cup of coffee in the machine and finished the cake. Yum Yum curled up on his lap, and Koko disposed of the crumbs on the carpet. Sirens sounded, speeding north on Main Street, and Qwilleran automatically glanced at his watch. It was 1:35 A.M.

The next morning he remembered the sirens when he tuned in the headline news on WPKX: "All dental appointments at the Zoller Clinic are cancelled today due to a fire that broke out sometime after one o'clock this morning. Arson is suspected, and police are investigating. Patients may call to re-schedule."

SCENE FOUR

Place: Qwilleran's apartment; later, the
       rehearsal hall
Time: Tuesday evening
Featuring: CHAD LANSPEAK

The Lanspeak department store closed at 5:30,
and Qwilleran wondered if Chad Lanspeak would
appear as promised. If he were as irresponsible as
Brodie thought, he would have forgotten about the
appointment and gone fishing. At 5:45 there was no
sign of the reputed black sheep. Qwilleran peered
out the window toward Main Street and saw only

the construction workers driving away in their trucks.

Finally at 6:15 a battered pickup turned into the driveway, coughing and shuddering as it came up to the carriage house, where it stopped with an explosive jerk. A young man jumped out and collected an armful of snowshoes from the truck bed. Qwilleran pressed the buzzer that released the door, and Chad Lanspeak struggled up the stairs with his load— gracefully shaped, honey-colored wood frames with a varnished sheen, laced with natural leather thongs in an intricate pattern.

"I brought 'em all," he said. "I didn't know I had so many. Hey, what's that iron thing?" He was staring at the Mackintosh insignia with the curious motto circling the rampant cats: TOUCH NOT THE CATT BOT A GLOVE.

"It came from the gate of a Scottish castle," Qwilleran said. "It's three hundred years old."

"It must be valuable."

"It has sentimental value. My grandparents came from Scotland."

Chad was hardly recognizable as the bored salesclerk at his father's store. He still sported the hirsute flourishes that made him conspicuous in Pickax, but he was as affable as any of the teens Qwilleran had met in that salutary environment. Country-bred youths, he had observed, possessed an easygoing, outgoing manner that bridged generation gaps.

"Line up the snowshoes on the living-room

floor," Qwilleran suggested, "so I can compare styles and sizes."

"I've never seen a place like this," said Chad, appraising the suede sofa, square-cut lounge chairs, chromium lamps and glass-topped tables.

"I like contemporary," said Qwilleran, "although it doesn't seem to be popular in Pickax."

"That's an interesting picture. What is it?"

"A print of an 1805 gunboat that sailed the Great Lakes."

"It has sails and cannon and *oars*! That's funny! A gunboat with oars! Where'd you get it?"

"From an antique shop."

"Is it valuable?"

"An antique is worth only what someone is willing to pay for it."

Next Chad admired the state-of-the-art stereo components on the open bookshelves, and Qwilleran began to think he'd made a mistake in bringing the fellow to the apartment. He thought, Dammit! He's casing the joint! The cats were present, quietly washing up after their evening meal, and Qwilleran spirited them away to their own apartment. Strangers often admired them less for their beauty than for their obvious monetary value, and it was his constant fear that they might be stolen.

"Now let's get down to business," he said. "I have a rehearsal at seven o'clock."

Chad was still attracted to the gunboat print. "There's a guy around here that makes model ships like that. He's really good. He could sell them for a lot of money if he wanted to."

"No doubt," said Qwilleran. "Now which style would you recommend for a beginner?"

"Let's see . . . the Bear Paw is easiest to start with, but it doesn't have any tail, and the tail helps in tracking, you know. I brought some bindings so you can see how they work. What kind of boots do you have?"

Qwilleran produced a pair of logger boots and was duly strapped onto a pair of Bear Paws. Awkwardly he attempted to maneuver them down the long hallway.

"You don't have to lift your feet so high," Chad called out after him. "Lean forward . . . Swing your arms . . . Your feet are too wide apart."

Qwilleran said. "I like the look of the others better. These remind me of fruit baskets."

"Well, there's this Michigan style; it's larger and has a heavier tail for tracking. The arctic is the fastest; it's long and narrow. All depends what kind of snow you have and how much brush. You should start with something smaller than those. Maybe you should try the thirty-six inch Beavertail."

Strapped onto Beavertails, Qwilleran clomped uncertainly down the hall again.

"Drag your tail!" Chad called out. "Your feet are too far apart. You'll get sore legs."

"It's like walking on tennis rackets."

"You'll get used to it when you get out in the snow."

"How much for the Beavertails?" Qwilleran asked. "I'll write you a check."

"It's hard to get a check cashed. Do you have the . . . uh . . ."

"I don't keep money in the house, but if you'll drive me to the east-side drug store, they'll cash a check for me. Then you can drop me off at the rehearsal hall."

He helped Chad carry the snowshoes down the narrow stairs and into the decrepit truck. It was a terrain vehicle, riding high on huge tires. As they started off, he remarked, "There's nothing wrong with this truck that couldn't be improved with a muffler, some springs, a coat of paint, and a new motor."

"It's okay," Chad explained. "It's what I need when I go setting my traps. Ever do any trapping?"

"I'm a city boy," Qwilleran said. "I don't trap or hunt or fish, but I know they're popular sports around Moose County."

"You can earn good money trapping. You can go shoeing with me when snow flies, if you want, and I'll show you how to use your Beavertails. Maybe you'd like to see my traps."

The idea of trapping wild animals repelled Qwilleran. He had heard that a beaver caught in the jaws of a trap would chew off its own leg to get free. Since he had shared living quarters with the Siamese he had become highly sensitive about cruelty to animals. Even the thought of hooking a fish disturbed him, although he enjoyed trout amandine at the Old Stone Mill.

"I'd appreciate a lesson in *shoeing* in actual snow," he said, trying to speak the lingo, "but I'm not sure I could warm up to the idea of trapping. Where do you go?"

"I get rabbits and squirrels in the Hummocks, and foxes out Ittibittiwassee Road. I use live traps mostly. That way the pelts aren't damaged."

Qwilleran stared ahead through the dirty windshield and said nothing. He didn't want to know what happened to the animals after they were trapped live.

"I got a skunk a couple of weeks ago. They're the trickiest. The safest thing is to drown them."

Qwilleran was glad when they arrived at the drug store. After the check was cashed and the Beavertails were paid for, they started off for the rehearsal hall with a rumble, a jolt, and a backfire, and he said casually, "What do you think of the vandalism in Pickax, Chad? It's getting pretty bad."

They had reached the main intersection and stopped for the traffic light—it was the only one in town—and Chad leaned out of the window and yelled "Hiya!" to the occupants of a noisy rustmobile. He didn't answer the question.

"When I was young," Qwilleran went on, "we used to overturn garbage cans in Chicago. For some strange reason that I can't remember at this stage of my life, we thought it was fun. What fun do they get out of breaking into the school and clobbering a computer?"

"I guess they didn't like school, and they're getting even," Chad said.

"And they didn't like having a tooth drilled so they set fire to the dental clinic. Is that the way it works?" Qwilleran asked him. "I don't understand it. You're young; maybe you can explain it to me."

"I wasn't anywhere near that place when it happened," Chad said defensively. "I was at a party in Chipmunk." He pulled up in front of the community center, jamming on the brakes hard.

"Thanks for the lift, fella. I'll get in touch with you when snow flies."

Chad nodded in sulky silence.

Qwilleran glanced at his watch; he was a half-hour late for rehearsal. The transaction had taken longer than he expected, and the detour to the drug store had wasted another twenty minutes. Francesca was strong on punctuality; she would not be happy.

When he walked into the rehearsal hall, the situation was worse than he expected. Several of the cast were absent without phoning in an excuse. Several, besides Qwilleran, had been tardy. Fran was vexed, and the general mood was tense. Reacting to her irritation the actors lost their concentration and missed their cues or fluffed their lines. In Qwilleran's vital scene he oozed up the stairway instead of charging like a madman. Eddington spoke his lines in a terrified stage whisper. The propman had forgotten to bring a sword, and Harley Fitch had never arrived with his grandfather's World War I bugle.

At one point the exasperated director waved them off the stage and tried coaching Eddington. The Lanspeaks took this opportunity to chat with Qwilleran. Larry said, "Our prodigal son paid us a surprise visit last weekend—in that truck he holds together with Band-Aids. He picked up all his snowshoes and said you wanted to buy a pair. He seemed almost human in spite of his alien genes."

Carol said, "And at the store today he was actually civil to customers. Everyone thought he must be sick."

It was the first time the Lanspeaks had ever mentioned their youngest, although they frequently boasted about the other two, who won math prizes, played the saxophone, captained the tennis team, and edited the yearbook.

Qwilleran said, "Chad brought the whole caboodle to my apartment and gave me a crash course in snowshoeing. I bought a pair of Beavertails."

"Quiet back there!" Fran shouted. "We're trying to rehearse." Later, when Carol got the hiccups and Susan got the giggles, she called out, "Break! That's all for tonight. We'll try again tomorrow, and if everyone isn't here at seven sharp, and if you don't know your lines and take the rehearsal seriously, there'll be no show!"

Qwilleran had never seen her so perturbed, and he mentioned the fact to Wally as they left the building.

"My mother would say it's because there's a full moon," said the taxidermist.

SCENE FIVE

Place: Office of the new Moose County
          newspaper
Time: Later the same evening
Cast: ARCH RIKER, publisher and editor
          in chief
          JUNIOR GOODWINTER, managing ed-
          itor
          HIXIE RICE, advertising manager
          ROGER MACGILLIVRAY, reporter

The stone buildings of downtown Pickax gleamed
blue-white in the light of the full moon. Following

the disastrous rehearsal, Qwilleran started to walk
home but detoured by way of the newspaper office.
It was the eve of the publication of the first issue,
and he was as nervous as a prospective father. At his
suggestion the Klingenschoen Fund had made the
venture possible. At his urging his longtime friend,
Arch Riker, had come up from Down Below to run
the operation. Eventually a printing plant and office
complex would be built; meanwhile, the paper was
being job-printed, and the editorial and business
functions were housed in a rented warehouse.

Qwilleran knew the staff had been working
twelve or more hours a day, and he had stayed out
of their way, but now it was the countdown; the
new publication would be in the hands of readers
Wednesday afternoon. He felt envious. It was a moment of excitement and tension, and he was an out-
sider.

As he expected, the lights were still on in the
building, a former meat-packing warehouse, and he
found Riker and Junior Goodwinter in the office
they shared—with beer cans in their hands and with
their feet propped on their desks. It was nothing
like the slick, color-coordinated, acoustically engi-
neered, electronically equipped work-station environment Riker and Qwilleran had known at the
Daily Fluxion. In this temporary situation execu-
tives and cub reporters alike sat at secondhand
desks and poked old manual typewriters in a
barnlike workplace that still smelled of bacon, al-

though Junior enjoyed the distinction of a rolltop desk that had been his great-grandfather's.

"The coffee's still hot," Riker said. "Grab a cup, Qwill, and find a chair. Put your feet up."

"Are you getting antsy?" Qwilleran asked.

"Everything's locked up except page one; we're still hoping for a banner headline for the kick-off. After the radio spots we got eighteen thousand subscriptions, and we've given a print order of thirty thousand. Hixie and her crew sold so many ads that we're going to forty-eight pages, twice what we expected."

Qwilleran had never seen him so animated. At the *Fluxion* Riker was the epitome of the jaded editor—a little paunchy, a little bored. Here, his ruddy face glowed with satisfaction and excitement.

The young, fresh-faced managing editor said, "We've got a lot of copy in type. Stories poured in from the stringers, but we still needed boilerplate to fill the holes. Roger MacGillivray quit his teaching job, and he's covering city hall, police, and general assignment. His mother-in-law is handling the food page; she teaches home ec, you know."

"I'm blissfully aware of her blueberry pies," Qwilleran said.

"Kevin Doone is writing a garden column for us. Do you know Kevin? He runs a landscape service."

"I know Kevin well. 'Call Doone to Prune!' I could live for a year on what he charged to prune a few apple trees on my property. Are you doing anything about the vandalism issue?"

"We're running a tough editorial," Riker said, "with a strong pitch for community involvement, parental responsibility, and more prowl cars after dark, even if they have to hire part-time officers. And the sheriff's got to keep an eye on those kids in Chipmunk. They think Pickax is a shooting gallery. It's time to turn off the indulgent grin and the sentimental attitude that boys will be boys."

"What happened at the dental clinic this morning?"

"They were apparently looking for narcotics and cash, and when they were disappointed they trashed the office and started a fire."

"I envy you guys. It's tough to be on the outside, looking in."

"I told you we could use your skills, Qwill," said Riker, "but you're busy writing that damned novel."

Qwilleran smoothed his moustache regretfully. "I'm beginning to think I'm miscast as a novelist. I'm a journalist."

"I could have told you that, you donkey!"

"And I don't have the temperament for free-lance work. I need the discipline of assignments and deadlines."

"Do you want to come on in?"

"What could I do?"

"Features. The kind of meaty, informative stuff you did for the *Fluxion*. We have a lot of space to fill and a lot of amateurs writing for it. We need all the professionalism we can get."

The front door slammed, and Hixie Rice suddenly appeared. "Quick, you guys! I need a beer, coffee, anything! I'm punchy! I've been hitting the restaurants all over the county. They all want to buy ads in the food section. These flat heels are *killing* me!" She kicked off her skimmers and turned to Qwilleran. "What are you doing here? You're supposed to be rehearsing or writing a novel or feeding your cats."

"If I haven't forgotten how," he said, "I'm going to write a column about interesting people who do interesting things."

"We're assuming," said Riker, "that such individuals exist in this outpost of civilization."

"There are no dull subjects," Qwilleran reminded him. "Only dull reporters who ask dull questions."

"Okay, so that's all settled! Now all we need is some hot-breaking news for page one. The opening issue is going to be a collector's item, and I want it to look like a newspaper."

Junior said, "Roger's at city hall covering the zoning-board meeting tonight, and if we're lucky, it'll break up in a fistfight, or something good like that."

"Don't you guys ever try any creative journalism?" Hixie taunted them. "Kidnap the mayor! Bomb city hall! Pull the plug on the Ittibittiwassee dam and flood Main Street!"

The three serious journalists scowled at her.

Qwilleran said to Riker, "What name have you picked for the paper?"

"That's got me stymied. I want it to be something like *Moose County Chronicle* or *Clarion* or *Crier* or *Caucus*. We've got to make a decision fast."

"You newspaper types have no imagination," Hixie objected. "Why not the *Moose County Cannonball* or *Crowbar* or *Corkscrew*?"

The three serious journalists groaned.

Qwilleran suggested, "Let the readers pick the name. Print a ballot on page one."

"But we've got to have some kind of flag for the first issue," Riker insisted. "We've got to call it something."

"Call it the *Moose County Something*," Hixie said. "I dare you!"

The front door slammed again.

"That's Roger," Junior guessed.

A young man with a camera bag slung over his shoulder burst into the office. Roger had a pale complexion and stark black beard, and tonight he was paler than usual. He was also breathing hard. He stared at the four waiting staffers.

"What's the trouble, Roger?" asked Riker.

He gulped. "Murder!" His voice cracked on the word.

"Murder?!" Riker took his feet off his desk.

"Who?" demanded Junior, jumping to attention.

"Where?" Hixie put her shoes on quickly.

"At city hall?" Qwilleran asked, touching his moustache nervously.

Roger gulped again. "In West Middle Hummock! Two people shot! Harley Fitch and his wife!"

SCENE
SIX

Place: The newspaper office
Time: The afternoon following the Fitch
murder
Cast: Staff members

The first copies of the *Moose County Something*
were coming off the press, and it should have been
a time of hilarity and popping champagne corks in
the city room, but the front-page news had dead-
ened everyone's spirit. In a small town like Pickax,
murder could not be an impersonal tragedy. Everyone was a friend or neighbor or relative or customer

77

of the victim. Even Arch Riker, relatively new in town and a veteran of a thousand, big-city murder stories, was gloomy. "I wanted a sensational banner for page one," he said, "but I didn't want it that bad."

A bundle of papers arrived from the job-printer and the staffers grabbed. Blazoned across the front page was the grim news: HARLEY FITCH AND WIFE FOUND SHOT TO DEATH.

In the cities Down Below, Qwilleran reflected, the public would immediately assume it to be a drug-related execution. In Pickax, 400 miles north of everywhere, there was no glimmer of such a thought. Suspicion might come later—in the coffee shops and over back fences—but at this moment the reaction was one of shock and sadness and reluctance to believe it could happen in Moose County.

Early that morning Francesca had phoned. "Oh, Qwill! Isn't it a beast! I've been nauseated all night. I heard it on the midnight news. Dad wouldn't talk about it. I suppose the paper will be out this afternoon with more details. I'd like to call David and Jill, but I'm afraid. They must be horrified."

"It's going to be on the front page," Qwilleran said. "It's the banner story with a picture of Harley. No one could find a photo of his wife—at least, not on such short notice."

"Downtown is crowded with people, all standing around talking about it. Nobody can believe it! With them expecting a baby and everything! Nobody can settle down to business."

"It's hard to take. Who could possibly have done it?"

"It's got to be the Chipmunk gang. The tourist season hasn't started yet; we don't have those crazies wandering around the county looking for something to shoot. Yes, it's definitely those punks from Chipmunk."

Qwilleran touched his moustache with his knuckles. "When everything went wrong at rehearsal last night I had a feeling there was something in the air. Wally said it was because of the full moon."

With a whimper Fran said, "And I was cursing Harley and David and Jill for being absent without explanation. Now that I know the reason, I could cut out my tongue. We'll cancel the show, of course. No one will have the heart to go on with it. God! I can't work. I can't do anything! I think I'll go home and drink up Dad's supply of Scotch. Do you want to come with me?"

The story on page one was subheaded: BURGLARY OBVIOUS MOTIVE. It carried the byline of Roger MacGillivray.

The scion of a prominent Moose County family and his bride of a few months were found shot to death Tuesday evening at their home in West Middle Hummock. Harley Fitch, 24, and his 21-year-old wife, Belle, were victims of a gunman whose apparent motive was robbery, according to the sheriff's department. The couple were preparing to leave the house for a Theatre Club rehearsal in Pickax, family members said. The time of death was between 6 and 7 P.M., according to the coroner.

David and Jill Fitch, Harley's brother and sister-in-law, discovered the bodies at 7:15 P.M., when they arrived to pick up the couple for the drive to Pickax. They live a quarter mile from the Fitch mansion, recently occupied by the newlyweds who were reported to be expecting a child.

Jill Fitch told police, "We've been rehearsing five nights a week for a play. We usually share the ride, leaving at 6:30. I tried to phone Harley to say we'd be a little late because of a plumbing problem, but there was no answer. I thought they were probably outdoors and couldn't hear the phone, so we just hurried as much as we could. When we finally drove up to their house, we tooted the horn, but no one came out, so David went in, and that's when he found them."

A spokesman for the sheriff's department noted that Harley's body was found lying in the rear entrance hall; his wife's body was in an upstairs bedroom. There was no sign of a struggle, the spokesman said. The two were wearing jeans and sweat shirts, described as "rehearsal clothes" by family members.

There was evidence, according to the spokesman, that the murderer or murderers had started to ransack the house and either found what they wanted or were interrupted by the arrival of the other couple.

Jill Fitch informed police, "I remember seeing a vehicle pulling away as we approached. It was going fast down the dirt road and throwing up a cloud of dust." There are no other residences on the road in question.

The 22-room house was the ancestral home of the Fitch family, built in the 1920s by Harley's grandfather, Cyrus Fitch, and noted for its valuable collection of art objects, books, and curios.

Harley was the son of Nigel and Margaret (Doone) Fitch of Indian Village. Following his graduation from Yale University and a year of travel, he joined the Pickax bank where his father is president. Harley and his brother, David, were recently named vice presidents.

Harley graduated from Pickax high school before attending Yale. He maintained a better-than-average scholastic record in high school while playing on the tennis team, participating in student government, and acting in student plays. In college he majored in business administration and continued his interest in the dramatic arts.

Upon returning to Pickax he was active in the Boosters Club and the Theatre Club, where he was last seen as Dromio in *The Boys from Syracuse*. He was an avid sailor, who skippered the 27-foot *Fitch Witch* to several trophies. A builder of model ships since the age of 10, he exhibited his handiwork frequently, winning numerous prizes.

Harley married Belle Urkle in October of last year in Las Vegas.

A sidebar carried comments from persons who had known Harley Fitch: the high-school principal, the tennis coach, schoolmates, the president of the Boosters, bank personnel, and Larry Lanspeak, representing the Theatre Club. "A model student . . . always enthusiastic and cooperative . . . fun to be with . . . talented actor . . . a 100-percent team player . . . wonderful to work for . . . always so thoughtful . . . upbeat all the way."

Qwilleran read the story three times, massaging his moustache as he read. There were details that aroused his curiosity. Down Below, when he was writing for the *Fluxion,* such an event would have demanded a bull session at the Press Club, with fellow journalists reviewing the story, analyzing, questioning, circulating rumors, airing suspicions, outguessing the police, exchanging inside information. Unfortunately there was no Press Club in Pickax, but he asked Arch Riker if he would like to have dinner at the Old Stone Mill.

For an answer Riker unlocked a desk drawer and withdrew a small box. He was looking smug. The box contained an impressive diamond ring. "I'm giving it to Amanda tonight," he said, his ruddy face virtually bursting with joy.

Qwilleran was nonplussed. This development accounted for Riker's uncharacteristically happy mien lately. Divorced after twenty-five years, he had been morose and introspective until he moved to Pickax, and Qwilleran was glad he had found a woman he liked. But *Amanda*! That was the shock.

"Congratulations," he managed to say. "This comes as a surprise."

"It will surprise Amanda, too. She's never been married, and we all know she's grouchy and opinionated, but what the hell! We're right for each other."

"That's all that matters," said Qwilleran.

Next he asked Junior to stay in town for dinner.

"I'm not a bachelor any more," said the managing editor with a happy grin, "and Jody's parents are up here from Cleveland to celebrate the kickoff. Jody's having leg of lamb and German chocolate cake."

Then Qwilleran broached the subject to Roger MacGillivray and offered to stand treat.

"Gosh, I'd like to," said Roger. "I don't often get a freebie. But Sharon's going to her cousin's bridal shower, and I promised to baby-sit. My life has changed a lot in the last couple of months."

Once again Qwilleran was the lonely bachelor surrounded by happy couples, and he thought regretfully of his failing friendship with Polly Duncan. There were others he could invite to dinner—Francesca, Hixie, Susan, even Iris Cobb—but none equalled Polly for stimulating conversation over the

duck à l'orange. And yet she had been noticeably
cool since he joined the Theatre Club and hired a
designer. Suddenly there had been no idyllic Sundays
at her little house in the country—no berry picking,
morel gathering, nutting, birding, reading aloud, or
other delights. Her chilliness was made more awkward by the fact that she was head librarian, and he
was a trustee on the library board.

In desperation he telephoned her at the office.
"Have you heard the news?" he asked in a somber
voice.

"Isn't it dreadful? Do they know who did it?"

"Not that I'm aware. No doubt the police have
suspects who are being questioned, but the authori-
ties aren't giving out any information. You can't
blame them. How have you been, Polly?"

"Fine."

"Could you have dinner with me tonight?"

She hesitated. "I suppose your rehearsal is canceled on account of . . ."

"The show is called off altogether, and I'm not
getting involved in any more plays. You were right,
Polly; they're too time-consuming. I'd like very
much to see you tonight."

There was a weighty pause, then: "Yes, I'd like to
have dinner. I've missed you, Qwill."

His sigh of relief was audible. "I'll pick you up at
the library at closing time."

He walked home with a light step, stopping at
Lanspeak's store to buy a silk scarf in Polly's favorite shade of blue, which he had gift-wrapped.

Returning home to shower and shave and dress for dinner, he bounded up the stairs three at a time, but lost his exuberance when the Siamese did not come to greet him. Where were they? He knew he had not locked them in their apartment. Mr. O'Dell had not been there to clean. He peered into the living room, but Koko was not on the bookshelves with the biographies, and Yum Yum was not curled up in her favorite chair.

Had someone broken in and stolen the cats? He rushed to their apartment. They were not there! He checked their bathroom. No cats! He called their names. No answer! In a panic he searched the bedroom. They were nowhere in sight. Were they shut up somewhere? He yanked open dresser drawers. On hands and knees he examined the back corners of the closet. He called again, but the apartment was silent as death. Fearfully he approached his writing studio. It was never tidy, but this time there were signs of vandalism: desk drawers open, papers scattered about the floor, desktop ransacked, paper clips everywhere!

It was then that he noticed two silent figures—one on top of the filing cabinet and the other on a wall shelf with *Roget's Thesaurus* and a bottle of rubber cement. Yum Yum was crouched on the shelf in her guilty position—a compact bundle with elevated shoulders and haunches. Koko was on the filing cabinet, sitting tall but without his usual confidence.

Qwilleran gazed down at the papers on the floor.

To his surprise they were all envelopes. *New* envelopes. His stationery drawer was open. When he scooped up the scattered items he noticed fang marks in the corners, and all the gummed flaps had been licked clean.

Sitting down in his desk chair he swiveled to face the culprits. He surmised that Yum Yum had opened the drawers with her famous paw, and Koko, who was attracted to any kind of adhesive, had been on a glutinous binge. Once before, he had ungummed a whole sheet of stamps, and had paraded impudently around the apartment with an airmail stamp stuck on his nose.

"Well, my friends," Qwilleran began calmly, "do I have to start locking my desk drawers? What's the mater with you two? Are you bored? Unhappy? Is there something lacking in your life? Is your diet inadequate?"

Koko, the usual spokesman for the pair, had no comment.

"You have epicurean food and the recommended daily allowances of vitamins. Do you realize there are cats who have to scrounge for their food in garbage cans?"

There was no reply.

"Has the cat got your tongue?"

Still no answer. Qwilleran doubted that Koko was even listening.

"You don't know how lucky you are. Some cats live outdoors all year in snow and sleet and torrential rains. You have a steam-heated apartment with private bath, TV, wall-to-wall carpeting, and . . ."

Qwilleran huffed into his moustache as the truth dawned upon him. Koko—with a glazed expression in his eyes and a peculiar splay-legged stance—was high on glue!

"You devil!" he blurted. And then he had a second thought. Koko never did anything unusual without a good reason. But what could this reason be?

y said, "She also had a deformed foot that
 her stagger and added to her inebriated image.
are your cats, Qwill?"
oko is happy that I've started collecting old
. He prefers biographies. How he can distin-
Plutarch's *Parallel Lives* from Wordsworth's
s is something I don't understand."
nd how is dear little Yum Yum?"
hat dear little Yum Yum has developed an un-
ant habit that I won't discuss at the dinner ta-

e ordered dry sherry for Polly and, for himself,
nk water with a dash of bitters and a slice of
n. (The village of Squunk Corners was noted
a flowing well, whose waters were said to be
apeutic.) Raising his glass in a toast, he said,
the memory of a promising young couple!"
Harley was an admirable young man," Polly
sadly.
Koko took an instant liking to him. No one
ns to know much about his wife. The paper said
were married in Las Vegas, and I thought that
sual. The affluent families around here seem to
big weddings at the Old Stone Church—with
lve attendants and five hundred guests and a re-
ion at the country club."
When David and Jill were married, their wed-
g cost a fortune."
Harley's wife never came to the Theatre Club,
the newspaper said both couples were going to

SCENE SEVEN

Place: Tipsy's Restaurant in North
 Kennebeck
Time: Later that evening
Introducing: POLLY DUNCAN
 MR. O'DELL, Qwilleran's part-time
 houseman
 LORI BAMBA, a friend of Koko and
 Yum Yum

When Qwilleran picked up Polly Duncan at the library he asked, "I'm glad you can have dinner with
me. Do you mind if we drive out into the country?

The bad news has made me restless and uneasy. I need to talk about it."

Her voice was soft and gentle, with a timbre that he found both soothing and stimulating. "I understand, Qwill. A tragedy like this makes people want to huddle together." She gave him a needful glance that was all too brief.

"I thought we might go to Tipsy's. Do you know anything about it?"

"The food is good, and it's very popular," Polly said brightly, as if determined to make this a cheerful evening. "Did you know the place was named after a cat? The founder of the restaurant was a cook in a lumbercamp and then a saloonkeeper. During Prohibition he went Down Below and operated a blind pig. After Repeal he came back up here with a black-and-white cat named Tipsy and opened a steakhouse in a log cabin."

"What was his name?"

"Gus. That's all I know. But he was legendary around here, and so was Tipsy. That was fifty or sixty years ago. The place has changed hands many times, but they always retain the name."

They drove through typical Moose County terrain: rolling pastureland dotted with boulders and sheep, dairy farms with white barns, dark stretches of woods, abandoned mines with the remains of shafthouses. At a fork in the road a signpost indicated that it was three miles to West Middle Hummock. The other branch of the road led to

Chipmunk (2 miles) and Nort⸻ miles).

"West Middle Hummock isn'⸻ munk, is it?" Qwilleran observed.

"A study in contrasts," Polly sa⸻

The highway soon ran through ⸻ standard dwellings: cottages with ⸻ and peeling paint, sheet-metal shack⸻ hardly larger than gypsy wagons, an⸻ advertising rooms to rent.

"The rooming houses were broth⸻ days of Chipmunk," she said.

Youths were hanging around the ⸻ and the party store, drinking from can⸻ the atmosphere with their boombox⸻ thought, Are these the rowdies who b⸻ school, trashed the dental clinic, and o⸻ drants? Is this where Chad Lanspeak ha⸻ the Fitch murderers holed up in this t⸻

North Kennebeck, on the other hand⸻ ing community with a grain elevator, ⸻ ums, an old railway depot conve⸻ museum, and Tipsy's—a log-cabin res⸻ attracted diners from all parts of the c⸻

The exterior logs were dark and chink⸻ rior was whitewashed and inviting, wit⸻ nishings and a casual crowd of dine⸻ spotlight in the main dining room hung ⸻ a white cat with black boots and a blac⸻ seemed to be slipping down over one ⸻ her the look of a tipsy matron.

the rehearsal and both couples were wearing rehearsal clothes."

Polly raised her eyebrows. "Did you ever read a news story that was completely accurate?"

They consulted the menu. It was no-frills cuisine at Tipsy's, but the cooks knew what they were doing. Polly was happy that her pickerel tasted like fish and not like seasoned bread crumbs. Qwilleran was happy that his steak required chewing. "I always suspect beef that melts in my mouth," he said.

The conversation never strayed far from the Fitch case. Polly worried about Harley's mother, who was a trustee on the library board. "Margaret has very high blood pressure. I'm afraid to think how she may react to the shock. She's such a wonderful person—so generous with her time, always willing to chair a committee or captain a fund-raising event—not just for the library, but for the hospital and school. Nigel is the same way. They're beautiful people!"

"Hmmm," Qwilleran mused, unsure how to react to this outpouring of sentiment—so unusual for Polly. "It will be rough on David," he ventured to say. "He and his brother were so close."

"Yes, and David was the more sensitive of the two, but Jill will give him the support he needs. She has a firm grip on her emotions. Did you notice that it was Jill who was quoted in the newspaper? When she and David were married, everyone in the wedding party was nervous except the bride."

"Didn't it surprise you to learn that we've had an armed robbery in Moose County?" he asked.

"It was bound to happen. Firearms are plentiful up here. So many hunters, you know, with rifles, shotguns, handguns. The majority are responsible, law-abiding sportsmen, but . . . these days anything can happen." She shot him a quick, inquiring glance. "I don't hunt, but I do have a handgun."

Qwilleran's moustache bristled. Her reserved personality, her gentle manner, her quiet voice, her matronly figure, her conservative dress—nothing suggested that she might have a lethal weapon in her possession.

"Living alone on a country road, I feel it's only prudent," she explained. "What's happening Down Below is beginning to happen here. I've seen it coming. I don't like it."

"Why don't you move into town?" he suggested.

"I've lived in that little house ever since Bob died. I adore my little garden. I like the wide-open spaces. I enjoy living on a dirt road and seeing cows in a pasture when I drive to work.

"Sometimes one has to compromise, Polly."

"Compromise doesn't come easily to me."

"I've noticed that," Qwilleran said.

Polly declined dessert, but he was unable to resist the lemon-meringue pie.

"Have you ever seen the Fitch estate?" he asked.

"Several times. When Margaret and Nigel lived in the big house, she gave a tea for the library board every Christmas. They have hundreds of acres—

beautiful rolling country with woods and meadows and streams and a view of the big lake from the highest hill. The mansion that Cyrus Fitch built in the 1920s is a large rambling place. They say he designed it himself. He was a militant individualist! An avid collector, too. Harley and David grew up there—among big-game trophies, rare books, Chinese-temple sculpture, medieval armor, and all the exotic things that people collected in the twenties if they had money. When David married Jill, his parents built them a modern house on the property. When Harley married, he and his bride moved into the mansion and his parents took a condominium."

"Can one drive into the property?"

"It's a private road, but there's nothing to stop anyone from entering."

"What is there to attract burglars? I can't imagine that the thieves were interested in rare books or mounted rhinoceros heads."

"There was jewelry handed down in the family. I imagine Harley's wife received some of it after they were married."

Qwilleran stroked his moustache thoughtfully. "I have a feeling the killer or killers had been there before."

When they left Tipsy's and started the drive back to Pickax in the first pink of the sunset, he asked, "How do you like the *Moose County Something*?"

"I rejoice that we have a newspaper once more, but the name is appalling."

"It's only temporary until the readers cast their ballots."

"I was surprised at the size of it."

"It will settle down to twenty-four pages as time goes on. They plan to publish Wednesdays and weekends until the new plant is finished, then go to five days a week. I'm going to write a feature column."

"What about your novel?" Polly asked sharply.

"Well, Polly, I've reached the painful decision that I'm not geared for producing fiction. For twenty-five years my career was based on ferreting out facts, verifying facts, organizing facts and reporting them accurately. It seems to have stultified my imagination."

"But you've been working on your novel for two years!"

"I've been talking about it for two years," he corrected her. "I'm getting nowhere. Maybe I'm just lazy."

"You disappoint me, Qwill."

"You overestimate me. You were expecting me to be a north-woods Faulkner or a dry-land Melville."

"I was expecting you to write something of lasting value. Now you will simply produce more disposable newspaper prose. Your columns in the *Daily Fluxion* were always well-written and informative and entertaining, but are you living up to your potential?"

"I know my limitations, Polly. You're setting a

SCENE SEVEN

Place: Tipsy's Restaurant in North
Kennebeck
Time: Later that evening
Introducing: POLLY DUNCAN
MR. O'DELL, Qwilleran's part-time
houseman
LORI BAMBA, a friend of Koko and
Yum Yum

When Qwilleran picked up Polly Duncan at the library he asked, "I'm glad you can have dinner with me. Do you mind if we drive out into the country?

89

The bad news has made me restless and uneasy. I need to talk about it."

Her voice was soft and gentle, with a timbre that he found both soothing and stimulating. "I understand, Qwill. A tragedy like this makes people want to huddle together." She gave him a needful glance that was all too brief.

"I thought we might go to Tipsy's. Do you know anything about it?"

"The food is good, and it's very popular," Polly said brightly, as if determined to make this a cheerful evening. "Did you know the place was named after a cat? The founder of the restaurant was a cook in a lumbercamp and then a saloonkeeper. During Prohibition he went Down Below and operated a blind pig. After Repeal he came back up here with a black-and-white cat named Tipsy and opened a steakhouse in a log cabin."

"What was his name?"

"Gus. That's all I know. But he was legendary around here, and so was Tipsy. That was fifty or sixty years ago. The place has changed hands many times, but they always retain the name."

They drove through typical Moose County terrain: rolling pastureland dotted with boulders and sheep, dairy farms with white barns, dark stretches of woods, abandoned mines with the remains of shafthouses. At a fork in the road a signpost indicated that it was three miles to West Middle Hummock. The other branch of the road led to

Chipmunk (2 miles) and North Kennebeck (10 miles).

"West Middle Hummock isn't far from Chipmunk, is it?" Qwilleran observed.

"A study in contrasts," Polly said.

The highway soon ran through a cluster of substandard dwellings: cottages with sagging porches and peeling paint, sheet-metal shacks, trailer homes hardly larger than gypsy wagons, and larger houses advertising rooms to rent.

"The rooming houses were brothels in the early days of Chipmunk," she said.

Youths were hanging around the burger palace and the party store, drinking from cans and blasting the atmosphere with their boomboxes. Qwilleran thought, Are these the rowdies who broke into the school, trashed the dental clinic, and opened the hydrants? Is this where Chad Lanspeak hangs out? Are the Fitch murderers holed up in this town?

North Kennebeck, on the other hand, was a thriving community with a grain elevator, condominiums, an old railway depot converted into a museum, and Tipsy's—a log-cabin restaurant that attracted diners from all parts of the county.

The exterior logs were dark and chinked; the interior was whitewashed and inviting, with rustic furnishings and a casual crowd of diners. Under a spotlight in the main dining room hung a portrait of a white cat with black boots and a black patch that seemed to be slipping down over one eye. It gave her the look of a tipsy matron.

Polly said, "She also had a deformed foot that made her stagger and added to her inebriated image. How are your cats, Qwill?"

"Koko is happy that I've started collecting old books. He prefers biographies. How he can distinguish Plutarch's *Parallel Lives* from Wordsworth's poems is something I don't understand."

"And how is dear little Yum Yum?"

"That dear little Yum Yum has developed an unpleasant habit that I won't discuss at the dinner table."

He ordered dry sherry for Polly and, for himself, Squunk water with a dash of bitters and a slice of lemon. (The village of Squunk Corners was noted for a flowing well, whose waters were said to be therapeutic.) Raising his glass in a toast, he said, "To the memory of a promising young couple!"

"Harley was an admirable young man," Polly said sadly.

"Koko took an instant liking to him. No one seems to know much about his wife. The paper said they were married in Las Vegas, and I thought that unusual. The affluent families around here seem to like big weddings at the Old Stone Church—with twelve attendants and five hundred guests and a reception at the country club."

"When David and Jill were married, their wedding cost a fortune."

"Harley's wife never came to the Theatre Club, yet the newspaper said both couples were going to

the rehearsal and both couples were wearing rehearsal clothes."

Polly raised her eyebrows. "Did you ever read a news story that was completely accurate?"

They consulted the menu. It was no-frills cuisine at Tipsy's, but the cooks knew what they were doing. Polly was happy that her pickerel tasted like fish and not like seasoned bread crumbs. Qwilleran was happy that his steak required chewing. "I always suspect beef that melts in my mouth," he said.

The conversation never strayed far from the Fitch case. Polly worried about Harley's mother, who was a trustee on the library board. "Margaret has very high blood pressure. I'm afraid to think how she may react to the shock. She's such a wonderful person—so generous with her time, always willing to chair a committee or captain a fund-raising event—not just for the library, but for the hospital and school. Nigel is the same way. They're beautiful people!"

"Hmmm," Qwilleran mused, unsure how to react to this outpouring of sentiment—so unusual for Polly. "It will be rough on David," he ventured to say. "He and his brother were so close."

"Yes, and David was the more sensitive of the two, but Jill will give him the support he needs. She has a firm grip on her emotions. Did you notice that it was Jill who was quoted in the newspaper? When she and David were married, everyone in the wedding party was nervous except the bride."

"Didn't it surprise you to learn that we've had an armed robbery in Moose County?" he asked.

"It was bound to happen. Firearms are plentiful up here. So many hunters, you know, with rifles, shotguns, handguns. The majority are responsible, law-abiding sportsmen, but . . . these days anything can happen." She shot him a quick, inquiring glance. "I don't hunt, but I do have a handgun."

Qwilleran's moustache bristled. Her reserved personality, her gentle manner, her quiet voice, her matronly figure, her conservative dress—nothing suggested that she might have a lethal weapon in her possession.

"Living alone on a country road, I feel it's only prudent," she explained. "What's happening Down Below is beginning to happen here. I've seen it coming. I don't like it."

"Why don't you move into town?" he suggested.

"I've lived in that little house ever since Bob died. I adore my little garden. I like the wide-open spaces. I enjoy living on a dirt road and seeing cows in a pasture when I drive to work.

"Sometimes one has to compromise, Polly."

"Compromise doesn't come easily to me."

"I've noticed that," Qwilleran said.

Polly declined dessert, but he was unable to resist the lemon-meringue pie.

"Have you ever seen the Fitch estate?" he asked.

"Several times. When Margaret and Nigel lived in the big house, she gave a tea for the library board every Christmas. They have hundreds of acres—

beautiful rolling country with woods and meadows
and streams and a view of the big lake from the
highest hill. The mansion that Cyrus Fitch built in
the 1920s is a large rambling place. They say he designed it himself. He was a militant individualist!
An avid collector, too. Harley and David grew up
there—among big-game trophies, rare books,
Chinese-temple sculpture, medieval armor, and all
the exotic things that people collected in the twenties if they had money. When David married Jill, his
parents built them a modern house on the property.
When Harley married, he and his bride moved into
the mansion and his parents took a condominium."

"Can one drive into the property?"

"It's a private road, but there's nothing to stop
anyone from entering."

"What is there to attract burglars? I can't imagine
that the thieves were interested in rare books or
mounted rhinoceros heads."

"There was jewelry handed down in the family. I
imagine Harley's wife received some of it after they
were married."

Qwilleran stroked his moustache thoughtfully. "I
have a feeling the killer or killers had been there before."

When they left Tipsy's and started the drive back
to Pickax in the first pink of the sunset, he asked,
"How do you like the *Moose County Something*?"

"I rejoice that we have a newspaper once more,
but the name is appalling."

"It's only temporary until the readers cast their ballots."

"I was surprised at the size of it."

"It will settle down to twenty-four pages as time goes on. They plan to publish Wednesdays and weekends until the new plant is finished, then go to five days a week. I'm going to write a feature column."

"What about your novel?" Polly asked sharply.

"Well, Polly, I've reached the painful decision that I'm not geared for producing fiction. For twenty-five years my career was based on ferreting out facts, verifying facts, organizing facts and reporting them accurately. It seems to have stultified my imagination."

"But you've been working on your novel for two years!"

"I've been talking about it for two years," he corrected her. "I'm getting nowhere. Maybe I'm just lazy."

"You disappoint me, Qwill."

"You overestimate me. You were expecting me to be a north-woods Faulkner or a dry-land Melville."

"I was expecting you to write something of lasting value. Now you will simply produce more disposable newspaper prose. Your columns in the *Daily Fluxion* were always well-written and informative and entertaining, but are you living up to your potential?"

"I know my limitations, Polly. You're setting a

goal for me that's unrealistic." He was becoming annoyed.

"It was your idea to write a novel."

"It's every writer's idea to write a novel sooner or later, but not all of us have the aptitude. On my desk I have a bushel of notes and a fistful of half-written pages." Unfortunately his voice was rising. "I need the discipline of a newspaper job! That's why I'm writing a column for the *Moose County Something*." His tone had a finality that implied: Like it or not!

Polly looked at her watch. They were nearing the center of Pickax. "I enjoyed having dinner with you."

"Won't you come up to the apartment for a night-cap?"

"Not tonight, thanks. I have things to do." Her voice was curt.

The last few blocks were driven in silence. With a brief good-night she transferred to her own car in the library parking lot—the cranberry-red two-door he had given her for Christmas during a surge of holiday spirit, grateful sentiment, and emotional de-lirium. When she drove away, the blue silk scarf in the gift-wrapped box was still on the back seat of his car, quite forgotten.

It was too good to last, he thought, as he drove around the Park Circle to his carriage house. His re-lationship with Polly was inevitably coming to an end. Once loving and agreeable, she had become critical. She thought their intimacy gave her license to direct his life, but he was his own man. That was why his marriage had failed a dozen years before.

As he unlocked the door of the carriage house, he heard the telephone ringing, and he ran up the stairs, hoping . . . hoping that Polly had changed her mind . . . hoping she had driven a few blocks and had stopped at a phone booth . . .

The voice he heard, however, was that of Mr. O'Dell, the white-haired houseman who had been school janitor for forty years and now conducted his own one-man janitorial service.

"Sure, an' it's sad news tonight," said Mr. O'Dell. "Young Harley was a good lad, but he married the wrong colleen, I'm thinkin'. Will yourself be needin' me tomorrow, now? It's a new grandson I have in Kennebeck, and the urge is upon me to lay eyes on the mite of a boy."

"By all means take the day off, Mr. O'Dell," said Qwilleran. "Was everything all right when you were here?"

"All but the little one. Herself did her dirty outside the sandbox again. It's bothered about somethin', she is."

Qwilleran immediately phoned Lori Bamba in Mooseville, the young lady who seemed to know all about cats. He described the situation. "Yum Yum has always had good aim until recently. I bought a second commode, thinking she wanted facilities of her own, but she ignores the pan and bestows her souvenirs on the bathroom floor."

"It might be stress," Lori said. "Is she under stress?"

"*Stress!*" he shouted into the phone. "I'm the one who's under stress! She lives a life of utter tranquility. She has a comfortable apartment with all conveniences—two gourmet meals every day, brushing three times a week. She has a reserved seat on my lap every time I sit down. And I hold intelligent conversations with both of them, the way you recommended."

"Have you made any recent changes in her environment?"

"Only new wallpaper in the living room. I don't see why that should concern her."

"Well," said Lori, "you should observe her closely, and if any other symptoms develop, take her to the doctor."

Qwilleran did not sleep well that night. It worried him inordinately when anything was wrong with the Siamese. He regretted also what was happening between Polly and himself. In addition, he could not help grieving about the cold-blooded murder that had gripped the community with sadness and fear. As he lay awake, he heard the 1:30 A.M. freight train blowing its mournful whistle at unguarded crossings near the city limits. The weather was clear, and, with his ear on the pillow, he could hear the dull click of wheels on tracks, although it was almost half a mile away. When the 2:30 A.M. freight rumbled through town, he was still awake.

SCENE EIGHT

Place: Downtown Pickax
Time: The day before the Fitch funeral

Qwilleran tuned in the headline news on WPKX every half hour expecting to hear that suspects in the murder of Harley and Belle Fitch were being questioned, or that arrests had been made and charges brought, or that the murderer had given himself up, or that he had killed himself, leaving a confession in a suicide note. Despite the scenarios he composed, nothing of the sort happened. It was reported only that police were investigating.

It also was announced that the funeral would be held on Friday, and it was the wish of the family that it be private. Qwilleran knew the decision would disappoint most of the local citizens; funeral-going and funeral-watching were consuming interests in Pickax.

Further, it was announced that Margaret Fitch, mother of the slain man, had suffered a massive stroke and was in critical condition at the Pickax hospital.

All of this only aggravated Qwilleran's impatience to know exactly what was happening, and he walked to the police station to confront Brodie—walking less briskly than usual; after a sleepless night he lacked pep. They had not talked together since the incident in West Middle Hummock, but Brodie would know everything and would be willing to reveal a few facts, off the record.

"Bad business, Brodie," Qwilleran said upon entering the office.

"Bad business," echoed the chief without lifting his eyes from his paperwork.

"Any suspects?"

"That's not for me to say. It's not my case."

"I suppose West Middle Hummock is the sheriff's turf."

Brodie nodded. "And the state police are assisting."

"Off the record, Brodie, do you suspect the punks from Chipmunk?"

The chief looked Qwilleran straight in the eye and said coolly, "No comment."

This was a surprising response from the usually talkative lawman, but Qwilleran knew when to stop wasting his time. "Take it easy," he said as he left.

His next stop was the office of the *Moose County Something*. In a newspaper city room one could always count on hearing inside information, true or false. He discovered, however, that Junior Goodwinter was taking a day off, having worked seven days a week since the inception of the project, and Roger MacGillivray was out on the beat, pursuing a story on wild turkeys.

Arch Riker was on hand, huddled over his desk, but he had heard no rumors and could answer no questions.

Qwilleran said, "I'm curious about the background of Belle Fitch. My houseman says Harley married the wrong woman."

"You hound-dog!" Riker exploded, pushing his chair away from his desk in an impatient gesture. "You're never happy unless you're sniffing the trail of something that's none of your business!"

Surprised by his friend's acerbic comment, Qwilleran said teasingly, "What's eating you, Arch? Did Amanda refuse your ring?"

"That's none of your business either," the editor snapped. "When can we have your first column?"

"When do you want it?"

"Tomorrow noon for the weekend edition."

This was the kind of short deadline that heated Qwilleran's blood, concentrated his attention, and primed the flow of ideas. "How about a piece on the eccentric bookseller who does business in a former blacksmith shop?"

"What about pix? Do you have a camera?"

"Not good enough to shoot dark books and a dark cat in a dark store."

"Okay, line it up, and we'll assign our part-time photographer—if we can find him—and if he can find his camera."

Qwilleran left the office with restored pep. About Riker's late-blooming romance he had ambivalent reactions, however. The two of them had grown up together in Chicago, and he would be sorry to see his friend disappointed. On the other hand, it would mean that Riker would still be available for bachelor dinners at the Old Stone Mill and bull sessions at the Shipwreck Tavern in Mooseville.

He picked up a tape recorder and a notebook from the city room and walked briskly to the store called Edd's Editions. The bell on the door tinkled, and Eddington Smith appeared out of the gloom.

"A terrible thing," the little man said in a voice denoting grief. "Is there any more news about the murder?" At that moment Qwilleran realized for the first time that the perpetual smile on the bookseller's face was a masklike grimace.

"The police are investigating," he said. "That's all

I know. Perhaps you heard that Mrs. Fitch has had a stroke. She's in critical condition."

The bookman shook his head sorrowfully. "I knew the whole family. It doesn't seem like it's really happening. 'All the world's a stage, and all the men and women merely players,' as someone said."

There was a tiny "meow" in a dark corner, and Winston came into view, waving his plumed tail and jumping across tables—from medical books to biographies to mysteries to cookbooks.

Qwilleran stroked the fluffy smoke-toned back. "I'd like to write a column about your enterprise for the new paper, Edd. In your ad you mentioned book repair. Is there much repair work in a town like this?"

"Not much. The library gives me some work, though. Mrs. Duncan is very nice. And this morning a lady from Sawdust City brought me a family bible to be repaired. She saw my ad."

"Where do you do this work?"

"My bindery is in the back. Would you like to see it?"

"Yes, and I'd like to turn on my tape recorder and ask some questions."

Eddington led the way into the back room, and Winston jumped off the cookbooks and followed.

"Did you ever see a hand bindery?" the bookman asked with a show of pride. He pulled cords dangling from the ceiling, and fluorescent tubes illuminated a roomful of bookpresses, cutting machines, a grindstone, workbenches, stools of varying heights, a small gas stove, and unusual tools.

Qwilleran started making notes on what he was seeing, and Eddington saw him staring at the small stove.

"That's for heating the glue," he said. "And my soup."

The two men perched on stools, and Eddington handed Qwilleran an open book. "Look at page seventy-two. I can repair a tear with transparent Japanese tape and some cornstarch paste, and the mend is invisible."

It was true. Page seventy-two looked flawless.

As Winston jumped onto the workbench where they were sitting, the bookman said, "He always comes into the bindery when I'm working. He likes the smell of glue and paste."

"Koko likes to sniff glue, too. What kind do you use?"

"Nothing synthetic. I make my paste out of wheat flour or cornstarch. The glue comes from animal hides. I buy it in sheets and melt it. Did you know it's the glue used in bookbindings that attracts bookworms?"

As Eddington talked about his craft, he was no longer the shy man who ran the bookshop with a soft sell and whispered his lines at the Theatre Club. He spoke softly but with authority and demonstrated book-binding operations with skilled assurance.

"How did you get interested in books?" Qwilleran asked.

"My great-grandfather was a book collector. You know the town called Smith's Folly? He founded it in 1856. His mine failed twice, but the third time he struck it rich."

"What happened to your great-grandfather's fortune?" Qwilleran asked as he glanced around the room. In the far corner there was an uncomfortable-looking cot, a folding card table with a solitary folding chair, a small sink with a mirror hanging on the wall above it, and a shelf of dishes and canned goods.

"I'm sorry to say the next generation spent it all on lovely ladies," said Eddington, blushing an unhealthy purple. "My father had to earn his living selling books from door-to-door."

"What kind of books?"

"Classics, dictionaries, encyclopedias, etiquette books—things like that. People with no education wanted to improve themselves, and my father was like a missionary, telling them to read and live better lives. He never made much money, but he was honest and respected. As somebody said, 'Virtue and riches seldom settle on one man.' "

"And how did you get into the used-book business?"

"An old man died, and they threw his books on the dump. I carted them away in a wheelbarrow. I was only fourteen. Now I buy from estates. Sometimes there's an odd book in the lot that's worth something. I found a first of Mark Twain in a box with some old schoolbooks and etiquette books. And once I found a book that Longfellow inscribed to Hawthorne."

"In your ad you mentioned library care as one of your services. What does that entail?" Qwilleran asked.

"If a customer has a good private library, I go and dust the books and treat the leather bindings and look for mildew and bookworms. Most people don't even know how to put books on a shelf. If they're too far apart, they yawn, and if they're too close together, they can't breathe."

"Are there many good private libraries in this area?"

"Not as many as before. People inherit them and sell the books to buy yachts or put their children through college."

"Could you name some of your clients?"

"Oh, no, that wouldn't be ethical, but it's all right to say that I took care of the Klingenschoen library when the old lady was alive."

"How about the Fitch mansion? Off the record." Qwilleran turned off the tape recorder. "I've heard they have some rare books."

Almost in a whisper the bookseller said, "Cyrus Fitch's collection is worth millions now. If they sell it at auction, it'll be big news all over the world."

"Do you suppose the burglars who shot the young couple were after rare books?"

"I don't think so. Not around here. Unless . . ."

"Unless what?"

"Oh, nothing. Just a silly thought." Eddington looked embarrassed.

"Are there professional book thieves—like the art thieves who steal old masters—who might come up here from Down Below?"

"I never thought of that. I should check the books against the inventory. But first I'd better talk to the lawyer."

Qwilleran asked, "How long have you been making house calls to the Fitch mansion?"

"Almost twenty-five years, and when Mr. and Mrs. Fitch moved out, they told me to keep on taking care of the library."

"So you knew Harley's bride. What was she like?"

Eddington hesitated. "She had a pretty face—very pretty. A little-girl face. I don't like to say anything unkind, but . . . she used to say some words that I wouldn't repeat even in front of Winston."

"What was her background?"

"Her name was Urkle. She came from Chipmunk. Of course, I knew her before Harley married her. She was one of Mrs. Fitch's maids."

Qwilleran remembered Mr. O'Dell's remark: "He married the wrong colleen." To Eddington he said, "One wonders why Harley would choose a girl of that class."

" 'Love makes fools of us all,' as Thackeray said. I *think* it was Thackeray," said the bookseller.

Qwilleran stood up. "This has been an enlightening session, Edd. A photographer will come around tomorrow to get a few shots."

"Maybe I'd better clean the front window."

"Don't overdo it!"

On his way to the exit Qwilleran stopped and asked, "When would you normally make your next house call to the Fitch collection?"

"Tuesday after next, but I don't know what to do now. I'll have to talk to the lawyer. I don't want to bother Mr. Fitch, but the books should be taken care of."

"I'd appreciate it if you'd take me along," Qwilleran said. "I might learn something."

"Shall I ask the lawyer if it's all right?"

"No, just take me along as your assistant. I'm good at dusting."

As Qwilleran walked home he marveled at the knowledge of the modest, self-educated little man, at his complete joy in working with books, and at his shabby living quarters. He remembered the narrow cot, and the sad table and chair, and the shelf above the sink. On it were a cup and plate, a dented saucepan, some canned soup and sardines, a razor and comb, and a *handgun*!

Arriving at his apartment he knew there was a message on the answer-box even before he reached the top of the stairs. Koko's mad racing back and forth told him the phone had been ringing in his absence.

The message was from Francesca. She would drop in at five o'clock. She had some stunning wallpaper samples for his bedroom. She also had some news, she said.

SCENE
NINE

Place: Qwilleran's apartment; later
Stephanie's restaurant
Time: The same day

Qwilleran went into his studio to organize his
thoughts and compose a catchy lead for the
Eddington Smith profile, taking care to confine the
cats to their apartment. Ordinarily they assisted his
creative process by sitting on his notes, biting his
pen and stepping on the shift key of the typewriter,
but this time he had a firm deadline. The Siamese
were banished.

The job required concentration. In his workshop Eddington used a strange vocabulary: giggering and glairing; nipping up, blinding in, holing out, wringing down and fanning over; casing in, lacing in, and gluing up.

Eddington had said that Winston liked the gluing-up process. Was Koko smelling the glue when he sniffed the spines of books as if reading the titles? Could a cat possibly smell the glue on a seventy-five-year-old volume of Dickens or a century-old Shakespeare? It hardly seemed likely. But, ruling out glue as the attraction, why did Koko sniff books? Why did he sniff certain titles and not others? Were there bookworms in the bindings? Could he smell animal matter? When they spent the summer months in the country, the Siamese were always fascinated by ants, spiders, and ladybugs on the screened porch. Why not bookworms? Qwilleran decided he would ask Eddington to inspect Koko's favorite titles. The cat had suddenly become interested in *Moby-Dick* and *Captains Courageous*.

These ruminations were not helping him meet his deadline, and when Francesca arrived with her wallpaper samples, he said, "Excuse me if I appear groggy. I've been working on a profile of Edd Smith, and I'm in a bookish fog. Tell me your news, Fran."

"First, a drink," she said, collapsing on the sofa.

"First the news," Qwilleran insisted, "and then a drink."

"Chad Lanspeak is a suspect! Carol and Larry are in a panic!"

"Hmmm," he said, tamping his moustache. "What time do the police think Harley was killed? Your father wouldn't tell me anything. I don't know why. Suddenly he clammed up."

"I know why," said Fran. "Last year he was reprimanded for talking about a case under investigation. Poor Dad! He loves to talk. I can probably find out for you. Why do you want to know?"

"Chad came to my apartment at 6:15 P.M. to sell me some handmade snowshoes. The transaction took longer than I expected, so it was 7:30 before he dropped me off at the community center. I know, because I looked at my watch and figured you'd give me hell for being a half-hour late. According to the newspaper account, David and Jill found the bodies at 7:15. Assuming Chad had put in a full day at the store, he couldn't be implicated."

"You should phone Carol and Larry and tell them that," said Fran. "They've called in their attorney. Do you know Hasselrich?"

"He's the attorney for the Klingenschoen Fund."

"Call Carol and Larry right away. It'll relieve their minds."

Qwilleran punched the number of the Lanspeak residence, visualizing their attractive country house as he waited for them to answer: split-rail fences, cedar shake roof, picturesque barn. "Hello, Larry? This is Qwill. I have some information for you that may be vital . . . Yes, I know. Fran told me, but assuming Chad worked a full day in the store, he's in the clear. He was with me from 6:15 to 7:30 and supposedly came directly from work. What time did he check out? . . . Well, then, he should be covered. You remember I told you he was selling me snowshoes. That's why I was late for rehearsal . . . That's right. He drove me downtown in his rattletrap truck and dropped me off at the rehearsal hall at 7:30 . . . Yes, I thought it might help. I even have a pair of Beavertails to prove it. Tell Hasselrich, and let him take it from there. I'm standing by if he wants me to do anything . . . So long, Larry. Chin up!"

As he poured Scotch for Fran, she walked around the living room, appraising it with a professional eye—moving a table three inches to the left, adjusting the blinds, straightening the picture of the 1805 gunboat. "How did this print get so crooked?" she asked. "We haven't had any earthquakes or sonic booms."

"Blame it on Koko," Qwilleran said. "He likes to rub his jaw against the corners of picture frames, and that one is easy to reach from the back of the sofa. If you knew anything about cats, that would be perfectly obvious."

She settled down with her drink. "I still can't believe we've lost Harley."

"No one says much about his wife. Did you know her very well?"

Fran shifted her eyes. "I met her a few times."

"Did she come from Chipmunk?"

"Somewhere out in that direction."

"What did people think about their marriage? Why were they married in Las Vegas?"

"Honestly, Qwill, I don't feel like talking about it. Harley isn't even buried yet. It's too painful. Mind if I smoke?" With gestures that had a practiced grace she shook out a cigarette, flicked the silver lighter he had given her for Christmas, and inhaled deeply.

Qwilleran waited for her to enjoy a few puffs before saying, "You and David were close friends, weren't you?"

"How did you know? It was just a high-school crush."

"Did you ever think you might marry him?"

"Did you ever think you might be a nosey bastard . . . *darling*?"

Archly he said, "I have a compassionate curiosity about my fellow beings. It's one of my noble traits." He produced a bowl of cashews and watched her gobble them hungrily. "Seriously, Fran, do you suppose the local investigators are competent to solve this case?"

"The state police have sent a detective up here, Dad says. A homicide expert. But don't underestimate our local cops. They've grown up here, and they know everyone. You'd be surprised how much they know about you and me and Chad and everyone else. They don't keep files on us; they just know."

Qwilleran poured another drink for her; her glass was emptying fast. "What's the Fitch mansion like?" he asked.

"Banana-split architecture at its gooiest!" she said. "A mix of Victorian Gothic, art deco and Italian. But it has a certain country charm. All those chimneys! All those rambling stone walls around the property!"

"I wonder if the killer or killers had time to find what they wanted before being interrupted. No doubt they had a lookout in their vehicle—someone who alerted them when David and Jill were approaching. What do you think they were looking for?"

"Money and jewelry, I suppose. They started ransacking the desk in the library and the dresser drawers upstairs. Harley's grandmother left jewelry in trust for Harley and David to give to their wives when they married. Belle had some pretty good things."

"What about books? Might they be looking for rare books?"

"Are you kidding? They were probably dropouts from Chipmunk who wouldn't know a rare book from a telephone directory."

"What kind of firearm did they use?"

"A handgun that's very common around here for hunting . . . Hey, don't let Dad know I'm telling you this. He's not supposed to discuss it, but he and Mother have a rap session at the kitchen table after every shift, and I have big ears."

"You have very lovely ears, if I may digress."

"Well, thank-you," she said amiably, looking surprised and pleased. "I just might go to dinner with you, if you extend the invitation."

"First I want to feed the cats," Qwilleran said. He released them and set out two bowls of the chef's *specialité du jour*, a kind of bouillabaisse without the mussel shells. "It would be interesting to know," he said, "if Harley knew the killer. I imagine it was someone who had been in the house and knew what they had. It was someone who knew their rehearsal schedule and expected them to be gone by 6:30. That is, if they were killed between 6:30 and 7:15. On the other hand, if they were killed before 6:30, it was by someone who picked a random time for robbery and murder."

"Qwill, this is giving me a headache. Can't we discuss the wallpaper and then go to dinner? Come over here and let's look at the samples."

They sat together on the sofa, with the heavy wallpaper book on their collective knees. The Siamese, meanwhile, had declined to eat; it was the same stuff they had been served for breakfast, and soupy concoctions were not their favorites. The two cats sat across from the sofa, staring into space.

Fran said, "I'd really love to see you do your bedroom in aubergine, avocado and rose taupe."

"I like it the way it is—tan, brown, and rust," Qwilleran informed her.

"Well, if you insist! How do you like this one? It's a marvelous texture in rust."

"The color's too dull," he said.

"Here's one with more life but not so much surface interest."

"Too flashy."

"How about this one?"

"Too dark."

"The wallcovering is only for the upper half of the wall," she reminded him. (The lower walls were paneled with the narrow wood beading common in nineteenth-century railway depots.) "In other words, it's simply a background for prints and watercolors that will be framed in chrome to tie in with your chromium exercise equipment. That is, if you're sure you want to keep the bike and rowing machine in your bedroom. Couldn't they go in the cats' apartment?"

Qwilleran scowled at her.

"Okay, they couldn't go in the cats' apartment. However," she went on, "I definitely think we should get rid of those ugly old-fashioned radiators. You owe it to yourself to install a completely new heating system."

"Those ugly old-fashioned radiators give good, even heat," Qwilleran said, "and they look right with the ugly, old-fashioned paneling. The plumber says they're over seventy-five years old and still in excellent operating condition. Show me any new invention that will still be good seventy-five years from now."

"You sound like my father," Fran said. "At least let me design an enclosure for the radiators—just a shelf on top and grillwork in front. My carpenter can build them."

"Will it impair their efficiency?"

"Not at all. I also think we should shop for new bedroom furniture for you when we go to Chicago. The new lines are coming out, and I have some wonderful sources . . . Ouch! . . . The cat grabbed my ankle."

"I'm sorry, Fran. Are your stockings torn?"

She smoothed her leg experimentally. "I don't think so, but those claws are like needles. Which one did it?"

Qwilleran watched Yum Yum the Paw slinking guiltily from the room. "Let's go to dinner," he said.

He gathered up Fran's wallpaper samples, and she dropped her cigarette pack into her handbag. "Where's my lighter?"

"Where did you leave it?"

"I thought I put it on the coffee table."

She rummaged in her handbag, and Qwilleran searched the floor and looked behind the sofa cushions.

"It can't have wandered very far," he said. "It'll turn up, and I'll give it back to you. Meanwhile, this would be a good time to give up smoking."

"You're sounding like my father again," she said with a frown.

They drove to Stephanie's, one of the best restaurants in the county. It occupied an old stone mansion in an old residential section of Pickax, and although the exterior was forbidding, the interior had a hospitable ambience created by soft colors, soft textures, and soft lighting. Qwilleran always liked walking into a restaurant with Francesca. On this occasion, heads turned to admire the young woman with gray eyes, gray suit, gray paisley blouse, gray hose, and high-heeled gray sandals.

Perusing the menu, he suggested the herbed trout with wine sauce.

"I'd rather have the spare ribs," she said.

"The trout is better for you."

"Will you stop sounding like my dad, Qwill?"

They talked about her father's virtuosity on the bagpipe, Qwilleran's fondness for things Scottish, Edd Smith's esoteric enterprise, and the future of the Theatre Club without Harley.

Qwilleran asked, "Do you know how David is reacting?"

"I talked to Jill on the phone, and she said he's a basket case. Nigel, too. I wonder if they're resilient enough to cope. They'll need counseling, that's for sure. To lose someone through illness or accident is traumatic, but murder is so evil!"

"Are you a good friend of Jill's?" He had observed a remarkable similarity between the two young women—their figures, their manner of walking and talking, their stagey Theatre Club gestures and attitudes.

"We were clubby in high school," she said. "We double-dated, played basketball, went in for art. She's very clever. I'm smart, I think, but Jill is clever."

"Is her family well-heeled?"

"Not any more. They lost everything in 1929. Her great-great-grandfather owned a string of sawmills. Her great-grandfather was a Civil War hero. Her grandfather was mayor of Pickax for twelve years. Her maternal grandmother . . .

As Francesca related Jill's family history, a scenario began to take shape in Qwilleran's mind. He waited a suitable interval before saying, "That was bad news about Harley's mother. Have you heard any more details?"

"No." The brevity of reply confirmed what he was thinking.

"If Mrs. Fitch doesn't pull through, it will be a great loss to the community. She's done so much for the public library, the hospital, the school, and other good causes."

Francesca's attention suddenly centered on her dinner plate.

"I've met Mrs. Fitch at library board meetings, and she impresses me as a very gracious woman—certainly generous with her time and cooperation."

Francesca raised her wrist and tapped her watch. "Do you realize what time it is? I've got to go back to the studio and write up some orders."

"And I have to buckle down to work on the Edd Smith profile." Later, as they said good night and she gave him a theatrical kiss, he presented her with the gift-wrapped silk scarf he had bought for Polly. "I know I'm a difficult client," he apologized, "but here's a small thank-you for your patience. And I'll have a good look for your cigarette lighter."

Upstairs in his apartment he found that the few remaining cashew nuts had been fished out of the bowl and batted around the room. "Is this your work, madame?" he asked Yum Yum, who was licking her right paw. "And do you know anything about a missing cigarette lighter?"

To Koko he said, "Fran wouldn't comment on Margaret Fitch, and she didn't want to talk about her relationship with David. Put two and two together and what do you get? A manipulative mother who stopped her son from marrying a policeman's daughter?"

"Yow!" Koko replied.

SCENE
TEN

Place: Qwilleran's apartment; later, the
newspaper office
Time: The day of the Fitch funeral

It was a private funeral in accordance with the
wishes of the family. The obsequies were held in the
Old Stone Church across the park from Qwilleran's
property, and the police kept traffic moving and dis-
couraged loitering in the vicinity. There were no
photographers waiting on the sidewalk or lurking in
the trees with their telephoto lenses.

Riker had wanted to give the event coverage, saying that Fitch was an important name in the county, the deaths were shocking, and the funeral was newsworthy.

Junior Goodwinter disagreed. "It's different in a town like this. We respect their feelings."

Riker insisted, and the argument became heated until Qwilleran was asked to mediate.

He agreed with Junior. "The public's right to be nosey won't be violated. Within an hour of the burial all the details of the funeral will be common knowledge. Telephones will be busy; the coffee shops will be buzzing. The Pickax grapevine is more efficient than any newspaper that publishes twice a week. So cool it, Arch."

On the morning of the funeral Qwilleran was typing the last paragraph of the Eddington Smith story and the Siamese were sitting on his desk when the telephone rang. Yum Yum flew away to parts unknown, while Koko jumped to the phone table and scolded the instrument.

"Qwill, this is Cokey," said the voice on the phone. Alacoque Wright, the young architect, sounded more mature than she had been during their brief fling Down Below. "I'm phoning from the construction shed on your front lawn."

"Good to hear your voice, Cokey. When did you arrive? How does the theater look?" Koko was now standing with his hind feet on the table and his forepaws on Qwilleran's shoulder, and he was snarling into the mouthpiece. Qwilleran pushed him away.

"The job is looking good. They've been following

the specs more closely this time. Only one problem: the wall color in the dressing rooms doesn't match the sample. It was supposed to be a rose ochre of low saturation to flatter the actors and elevate their mood. It will have to be repainted at the contractor's expense."

"How long are you going to be here, Cokey?" Koko was biting the phone cord, and Qwilleran gave him another shove.

"Until tomorrow noon. I'm staying at the Pickax Hotel. It's not exactly the Plaza, but my room has a bed and indoor plumbing, for which I'm grateful."

"Let's have dinner tonight. Come to my apartment over the garage whenever you're through with your work. We'll have a drink, and you can say hello to Koko. He's making an unholy fuss at the moment for some obscure reason."

"See you later," she said.

Qwilleran turned to the cat sitting on the phone table just beyond arm's reach. "Now, what was that all about, young man? If you must monitor my phone calls, try to act with civility."

Koko scratched his ear with infuriating nonchalance.

Qwilleran returned to his typing, only to be interrupted by a phone call from Polly Duncan. The dulcet quality of her voice indicated that she had recovered from her peevishness, and his hopes soared.

"I'm embarrassed, Qwill," she said. "Monday was your birthday, and I didn't even mention it when we had dinner on Wednesday. If it isn't too late to celebrate, would you be my guest at Stephanie's this evening?"

"I'd like that," he said with warmth. "I'd like that very much, but unfortunately the architect for the theater project is here from Cincinnati, and I have to do the honors."

"How long will he be here?"

"Uh . . . until tomorrow noon." He decided not to point out the gender discrepancy.

"Then could you dine with me tomorrow evening?"

"Saturday? That's when the newspaper bosses are treating the staff to a victory bash. It's just an in-house celebration with drinks, bonuses and speeches, but I have to be there to represent the Klingenschoen Fund."

"You're really keeping busy, aren't you?" she said crisply.

He waited hopefully for an invitation to roast beef and Yorkshire pudding at her cozy little house on Sunday, but she merely signed off with polite regrets.

So Qwilleran was in a sober mood when he walked downtown to hand in his copy and photo request at the newspaper office. As he approached the building he saw a post-office vehicle parked at the curb and a mailcarrier dragging large sacks into the building. Their contents were being dumped on the floor in the middle of the city room, and everyone—publisher included—was slitting envelopes and counting ballots for the official name of the new publication.

"Come on, Qwill!" Junior called out. "Dig in and start counting. Help yourself to coffee and doughnuts."

Hixie said, "The write-ins are the best. Here's one for *The Moose County Claptrap*."

By noon there were a few scattered votes for *Chronicle*, *Clarion* and *Caucus*, but 80 percent of the readers wanted to retain the flag used on the first issue: *The Moose County Something*.

"At least it's different," Riker acknowledged reluctantly.

"People around here like to be different," Junior explained. "My next-door neighbor hangs his Christmas tree upside down from the ceiling, and there's a restaurant in Brrr that charges a nickel for a paper napkin."

Roger said, "I know a farmer in Wildcat who doesn't believe in daylight saving time. He refuses to move his clock ahead, so he's an hour late for everything all summer."

"Okay, how about this one?" Hixie said. "I sold an ad to a little old lady in Smith's Folly who sells candy, cigarettes, and pornographic magazines, and she mentioned the Fitch funeral. She said she'd never been to a funeral. She said all her family were buried in the backyard *without any fuss*."

Riker said, "I don't believe a word of this nonsense."

"In Moose County I'll believe anything," Qwilleran said, "but Hixie is exaggerating about the magazines. I've been in that shop."

"It's true!" she insisted. "The racy stuff is behind a curtain."

"Okay, you loafers, back to work," Riker ordered. "Here comes the mailgirl with another sack."

Qwilleran wanted to leave, until he heard they were sending out for deli sandwiches. "What news on the police beat?" he asked Roger.

"The investigation continues. That's all they'll say."

"That's all they ever say. Have you had any tips that they're closing in?"

"Well, everyone seems to think it's narrowing down to Chipmunk. That's what people said from the very beginning. You know, I hate to see a town get a reputation like that. When I was teaching, I had some good students from Chipmunk. There are decent working-class families living in those low-rent houses, but a few hoodlums give the town a black eye."

Qwilleran was smoothing his moustache, and Riker noticed the familiar gesture. "If the police can't solve the case, leave it to Qwill," he said with mild sarcasm.

"One thing I've been wondering," Qwilleran said. "Harley's wife never attended rehearsals at the Theatre Club. Didn't like the people, I guess. So why was she going to attend on Tuesday night?" He waited for an opinion, but none was forthcoming.

"Did she want to be out of the house? Did she know what was going to happen?"

"Wow!" said Junior. "That's a pretty radical idea."

"We don't know what connections she might have had in Chipmunk. She might have collaborated in a plot to burglarize the house."

Roger said, "Her maiden name was Urkle, and they're not a bad family. Belle wasn't a good student; in fact, she dropped out. But she wasn't a bad girl."

"Go ahead, Qwill. What's your theory?"

"Let's say she supplied a key to the house and told her accomplices where to look for loot. But the timing was off, because David and Jill were delayed. When her confederates arrived, they were confronted by Harley. Maybe he recognized them, or maybe they were just trigger-happy and afraid he would identify them, so they killed him. Then Belle had to be silenced because she knew who had murdered her husband, and they feared she might crack under questioning."

"Wow!" said the young managing editor.

"How many do you think were involved in the break-in?" Roger asked. "Everyone refers to murderers, plural."

"In any conspiracy, the fewer the better. I would say there was one to stand look-out in their vehicle, and another for the inside work. Being alone, he might have been overpowered by Harley, so he had to shoot . . . I get a sad picture of poor little Belle

Urkle in her so-called rehearsal clothes, waiting upstairs, realizing the plot has failed, playing a scene she never rehearsed."

"Shall we have soft music in the background?" Hixie suggested.

"She hears the shot downstairs. She's terrified, not knowing what will happen next. She hears the killer coming up the stairs . . ."

"You'd better go back to writing your novel, Qwill," said Riker.

Then Roger said, "One of the cops told me something interesting today—off the record, of course. In determining the time of death, they decided that Belle was shot first."

SCENE ELEVEN

Place: The Old Stone Mill
Time: Evening of the same day
Introducing: ALACOQUE WRIGHT, architect from Cincinnati

While waiting for Alacoque Wright to arrive, Qwilleran wrote two letters of condolence: one to Nigel Fitch on the loss of his son, and one to David and Jill on the loss of their brother. He had to work fast in order to seal the envelopes and affix the stamps before that maniac of a cat swooped in with his wet tongue. As soon as an envelope or stamp came out of the desk drawer, Koko stalked it with a quivering nose and an insane gleam in his eye.

Next, Qwilleran prepared for company. He straightened the gunboat picture over the sofa, removed used coffee cups and scattered newspapers, put on his best suit, and filled the ice bucket with cubes. "Cokey is coming," he said to the Siamese. "Try to be on your best behavior."

Koko made an ugly noise, halfway between a hiss and a snarl, and Qwilleran suddenly realized why. At that moment the doorbell sounded, and Cokey was admitted.

There were hugs and kisses appropriate under the circumstances, and then Qwilleran said, "I can't call you C-o-k-e-y any more. Koko will have a fit. He thinks it's his name being spoken. Cats are jealous of their names. Koko doesn't like anyone to touch his tail, pry open his mouth, or apply his name to any other entity—animal, vegetable or mineral. That's why we have only ginger ale around the house and not that other popular beverage."

"That's all right," said Alacoque. "Call me Al. That's what my husband always called me. How are you, Qwill? You're looking so healthy, it's indecent. I missed you the first time I was in town."

"I was Down Below, partying at the Press Club, inhaling polluted air and trying to get unhealthy again, so my old friends would recognize me."

"I must say there's something about country living that agrees with you."

"You've changed, too," Qwilleran said. "You're

looking older and wiser, if you don't mind the dubious compliment." Formerly addicted to clothes that she made out of drapery samples, she was now the sleek, well-dressed, self-assured, city-bred, successful career woman—in pantdressing suitable for climbing around a construction site.

"There's nothing like a good job and a bad marriage to make a girl look older and wiser," she admitted ruefully.

"I didn't know about your marriage. Are you divorced?"

"No, but I work in Cincinnati, and he's driving a truck in San Francisco, where he belongs."

She volunteered no details, and Qwilleran asked no questions. Walking to the small serving bar incorporated in the bookshelves, he remarked, "I suppose you're still drinking yogurt and prune juice."

"Lord, no! I'll take Irish neat, if you have it . . . Is that Koko? He looks older and wiser, too."

"The little one is Yum Yum. You've never met her."

"She's adorable. How's your current love life, Qwill?"

"I don't know, frankly. I've been rather happy with a woman of my own age—a librarian—but she's beginning to resent the young woman I've hired as my interior designer."

"Stick with the librarian, Qwill. You know how I feel about interior designers! Remember when I was a reluctant assistant in Mrs. Middy's studio with all those calico lampshades and mammy rockers?"

Alacoque looked around the living room with approval. "I'm glad to see you've furnished in contemporary."

"I find it comfortable, especially with a few old books and old prints thrown in."

"Do you like living up here?"

"To my surprise, yes. I've always lived in big cities and had the big-city viewpoint, but people up here think differently and I find myself adjusting. Also, a town of this size has a human scale and a slower pace that I find comforting."

"That's the second time in a minute and a half that you've mentioned comfort. Is that a sign of growing older?"

"Older and smarter. In Pickax I walk a lot; I've lost weight, and I'm breathing better. We have fresh air, safe streets, minimal traffic, friendly people, boating in summer, skiing in winter . . ."

"Does Pickax need an architect? Young, talented, friendly female wishes to apply."

"I may need an architect soon," Qwilleran told her. "There's an old apple barn on my property that I'd like to convert into a place to live."

"I've always wanted to convert a barn."

"We're dining tonight at an old gristmill converted into a restaurant. I think you'll approve of it—both the food and the architecture. But first I'd like to give you a scenic tour of Moose County, whenever you're ready."

"Let's go," she said, draining her glass.

*   *   *

As they drove past farms, woods, lakes, and historic mine sites, Alacoque exclaimed over the grotesque shapes of weathered shafthouses, the stark remains of ghost towns, picturesque stone farmhouses, and a whole town of chinked log buildings on the lakeshore.

"And now we're coming into the Hummocks," Qwilleran said, "where the affluent families have their estates." The road swooped up and down nobby hills traced with miles of low, stone walls. Then he turned into a gravel road between stone pylons, marked PRIVATE. "This is the Fitch estate—hundreds of acres, in the family for generations. I've never been here before, but they say there are two interesting houses. One is a twenty-two-room mansion built in the twenties, and the other is a contemporary house that's been photographed for a national magazine."

The road curved around hills, ascended the rounded crests and dipped down again, winding between woodland and meadow.

"Gorgeous terrain!" Alacoque said. "Was it done by glaciers or bulldozers?"

They crested a hill, and suddenly in the valley below there appeared a sprawling stone house with many chimneys—and two police cars in the driveway.

"There was a murder here on Tuesday," Qwilleran explained.

"Was it a young banker and his wife?" Alacoque

asked. "I heard the construction workers talking about it."

A sheriff's car backed out of the drive and blocked the road as Qwilleran approached, and a brown-uniformed deputy strolled over to speak to him. "This road is closed, sir. May I see your driver's license?" He glanced at the wallet Qwilleran offered, and his expression relaxed as he recognized the name and photograph of the richest man in the county. "Were you looking for someone, sir? There's no one here, and no one at the other house, either."

"My passenger is an architect from Cincinnati," Qwilleran replied. "She's merely interested in seeing the exterior of David Fitch's house. Its architecture has had national attention."

"I see," said the deputy slowly, as he thought about it, bobbing his head until the tassels on his broad-brimmed hat danced. "You can drive up there if you want to. I'll lead the way. There are some tricky forks in the road and some muddy spots."

The two cars proceeded slowly along the winding road. "Muddy spots!" Qwilleran said. "It hasn't rained for a week." There were no forks in the road, either.

Up and down the gentle hills they moved until the spectacular house came in view.

"Fantastic!" Alacoque cried. "It's inspired by those shafthouses at the old mines!"

The contemporary house was built of rough cedar. Five cubes, each smaller than the one below, were stacked to make an irregular five-story pyramid, until the top floor was merely a lookout over the valley below.

The sheriff ambled over. "You can walk along the terrace if you want to. It has a good view. You can see the big lake from here."

"Do you know who did the construction?" Alacoque asked.

"Caspar Young, ma'am."

"Do you know who designed it?"

"No, ma'am."

As she studied the house from all angles, she remarked on the use of massive timbers, the cantilevered decks, the integration with the terrain, the fenestration, massing and site orientation, the planes and angles and voids. The deputy, who accompanied them closely, appeared to be impressed.

Qwilleran thanked him and then followed the official car back down the road. He looked at his watch. "I want to see," he said to Alacoque, "how long it takes to drive from here to the stone house, and exactly when and where it comes into view. I'm wondering how much warning the burglars had— how much time to pack their loot and make a getaway. David and Jill were late in picking up Harley and Belle. They said they had a plumbing emergency. If they had been on schedule, all this might not have happened. Did someone want them to be late? Was the plumbing emergency contrived?"

"I suspect the plumber," Alacoque said. "All plumbers look furtive to me."

The tour continued through Squunk Corners, the

lakeside town of Brrr, and Smith's Folly. Then they arrived at the Old Stone Mill, and Alacoque was enchanted by the former gristmill built of stone and nestled in a wooded setting. The old millwheel turned and creaked and shuddered as if it were still supplying power to grind wheat and corn. Within the building, timbers and floors were artfully bleached to the color of honey, and pale-oak tables and chairs contributed to the cheerful feeling of well-being.

"Hello, Derek," Qwilleran said to the tall busboy who was filling the water glasses with the air of one who owned the place. "You seem to be busy tonight."

"Friday, you know," Derek explained. "How did the cats like the poached salmon this morning?"

"It was a big hit! They even ate the capers." Turning to his guest Qwilleran said, "This is Derek Cuttlebrink, purveyor of fine foods to Their Majesties, the Siamese, and a member of the Theatre Club."

"Hi!" said the busboy.

"My guest has come all the way from Cincinnati to try your famous poached salmon, Derek."

"I have a cousin in Cincinnati," he said.

"Cincinnati is full of cousins," Alacoque said with a disarming smile.

Qwilleran asked, "Where's my favorite waitress tonight?"

"She quit. We have a new girl at this station. This

is her first day. She's pretty nervous, and she's kinda slow, so give her a break."

Eventually a thin, frightened girl presented herself at the table. "I'm S-s-sally, your s-s-server. Today's s-s-specials are clam chowder, oysters Rockefeller, and poached s-s-salmon. Would you like s-s-something from the bar?"

"Yes, Sally," Qwilleran said. "The lady will have Irish whiskey neat, and I'll have Squunk water with a dash of bitters and a slice of lemon."

"S-s-quunk water with . . . what?"

"A dash of bitters and a slice of lemon."

Alacoque was eager to talk about the theater—the two graceful stairways in the lobby, the rake of the amphitheater, the versatility of the staging area. "How good is your theater group?" she asked.

"A cut above most amateur companies," he said. "It was founded a hundred years ago and named the Pickax Thespians, but the present generation thought it sounded like deviant sex, so it was changed to the Theatre Club. The young man who was killed Tuesday was one of our best actors."

"What were the circumstances?"

"He and his wife were gunned down in their home—the stone house where we encountered the police cars."

"Were they into drugs?"

Qwilleran gave her a frigid glance. "No one is into drugs up here, Alacoque."

"That's what *you* think. Do they know who killed them?"

"They've been questioning suspects. Robbery was the obvious motive. They say the house is crammed with valuable collectibles, accumulated a couple of generations back. The family has old money, and they're very well liked. Harley and his brother have always been known as cooperative, outgoing guys with a lot of class."

"How about Harley's wife?"

"They'd been married only a short time. I never met her."

"I don't know whether I should repeat this, but . . . the construction gang said she was a tramp."

"Did they offer any corroborative detail?"

"No, but they all nodded and leered. Why would a man like Harley marry a girl with that reputation?"

"Pertinent question. I've been wondering about that myself."

Her attention was wandering. She said, "There's a woman over there who keeps looking at us. She's with another woman."

"Describe her."

"Middle-aged, intelligent looking, neat hair, pleasant face. Hair slightly gray. Plain gray suit, plain white blouse."

"Size 16? Walking shoes? That's my librarian," he said. "I told her I was having dinner with an architect from out of town, and she assumed you wore a beard and smoked a pipe. I didn't correct her. Now I'm in the doghouse for keeps."

"If you need consoling," Alacoque said, "young, talented, friendly female architect wishes to apply."

Suddenly there was a change of mood in the restaurant. The pleasant hum of diners' voices was interrupted by an excited hubbub in the rear of the room. The doors to and from the kitchen were rapidly swinging in and out. Waitresses were whispering to their customers, who responded with little cries of emotion and shocked exclamations. One waitress dropped a tray on the hardwood floor. It was Sally, who fell to her knees, frantically scooping up cheesecake.

Qwilleran flagged down the busboy. "What's happening here?"

"Sally heard the news and got all shook up, I guess. Lucky it was cheesecake and not soup or something."

"What news?" Qwilleran demanded.

"Did you know Harley's mother was in the hospital?"

"Of course I knew that," Qwilleran snapped impatiently.

Derek glanced toward the kitchen. "Our salad girl's mother is a nurse at the hospital. She just phoned and said Mrs. Fitch died."

"Oh, my God," Qwilleran moaned. To Alacoque he explained, "Mrs. Fitch had a massive stroke after her son was murdered."

"Yeah," said Derek. "Her husband was there at the hospital when she died, and he went out to the parking lot and sat in his car and shot himself."

SCENE TWELVE

Place: Editorial offices of *The Moose County Something*

Time: Saturday evening

The readers had given their mandate. With the publication of the weekend issue, *The Moose County Something* became the official name of the newspaper, although the decision grated on Arch Riker's better judgment and caused him acute embarrassment. He said, "I always wanted to be an editor in chief, but I never wanted to be editor in chief of something called *The Moose County Something*! Al-

145

ready I'm getting the raspberry—by mail, phone, and carrier pigeon—from the guys Down Below, and I'm afraid it's only the beginning."

Nevertheless he hosted the victory celebration on Saturday night with gracious hospitality. Desks in the city room were pushed together to serve as a bar and a buffet, and the former was dispensing everything from beer to champagne. Milling around the open bar were editors, reporters, columnists, one part-time photographer drinking enough for three, stringers from outlying towns, office personnel, adpersons, and the circulation crew.

Although exhausted after putting together the first forty-eight-page *Something,* the staff had managed to produce a weekend issue of thirty-six pages. It had gone to press too soon, however, to cover the deaths of Margaret and Nigel Fitch, and the banner headline on page one read: WILD TURKEYS RETURN TO MOOSE COUNTY.

Kevin Doone, who had been a pallbearer at the funeral of Harley and Belle, was doing justice to the open bar. "I need this," he said to Qwilleran, raising his martini glass. "Carrying that casket was the hardest thing I've ever had to do. Harley was my cousin, you know, and a super guy! When Brodie started playing the bagpipe as we were coming down the church steps, I really fell apart! David wanted a piper at the church and the cemetery because Harley always liked that kind of music. God! It sounded mournful! And now Aunt Margaret's gone. And Nigel! . . . I've got to get a refill."

Kevin dashed away to the bar, and the writer of social news, Susan Exbridge, caught Qwilleran's eye. *"Darling, why are we here?"* she cried, waving her arms and spilling her drink. Since getting a divorce and joining the Theatre Club she had become overly dramatic. "We should all be at home, privately mourning for Nigel—that beautiful man!"

Qwilleran agreed that the bank president was distinguished looking: tall, straight, perpetually tanned, with polished manners and affable personality. "How could he do it?" he asked Susan.

"He couldn't face life without Margaret," she said. "They were devoted! And, of course, everyone knows that *she* made him a success. He was a sweet man, but he would have been nothing without Margaret's push. She directed the whole show."

Qwilleran, carrying his glass of ginger ale on the rocks, moved amiably among the convivial drinkers, all complimenting each other on their contributions to the new paper. One of them was Mildred Hanstable, the buxom teacher from the Pickax high school, where she taught art and home economics, directed the senior play, and coached girls' volleyball. Now she was writing the food pages for the *Something*.

Qwilleran said, "Mildred, I read every word of your cooking columns, even though cubing and dicing and mincing are Greek to me. Everything sounded great, especially the Chinese chrysanthemum soup."

"When are you going to learn to cook, Qwill?"

"Sorry, but I'll never have the aptitude to boil an egg, understand an insurance policy, or file my own tax return."

"I could teach you to boil eggs," she said with her hearty laugh. "I give private lessons!"

Qwilleran's expression changed from genial to doleful. "This was the night there was supposed to be a house-warming party for Harvey and Belle. Tell me something, Mildred. Teachers and cops in small towns know everything about everybody. What do you know about Belle Urkle?"

"Well, I'm sorry to say she dropped out of school. She said she wanted to work for rich people and live in a big house. You could hardly blame her, if you'd seen how people live in Chipmunk. She was a maid in the Fitch house, but I can't understand what notivated Harley to marry her."

"Love? Lust? Biological entrapment?"

"But he didn't have to marry her and embarrass the family, did he? As soon as I heard about the murders, I got out the tarot cards and did a couple of readings. There's a deceitful woman involved!"

"Hmmm," Qwilleran said politely. He was skeptical of tarot cards. "May I replenish your drink, Mildred?"

When he returned with her Scotch and his ginger ale, he inquired casually about Harley's scholastic record.

"Both boys were good students—and so talented!" she said. "David did excellent pen-and-ink sketches, and Harley built model ships with exquisite detail. They were both in school plays, and I guess they became quite serious about drama in college. You may not know this, Qwill," she said, stepping closer, "but Harley disappeared for a year!"

"What do you mean by that?"

"Both boys were expected to come home after graduating from Yale—to work in the bank. Harley didn't show up."

At that moment Junior Goodwinter interrupted. "Don't you guys want any food? We've got turkey and corned-beef sandwiches."

"We'll be right there," Qwilleran assured him. "Mildred is divulging some cooking secrets."

"I always put a teaspoon of bitters in my lime pie," she said, picking up her cue, and when Junior moved away she said to Qwilleran, "No one really knows what happened to Harley. The family said he was traveling for a year, but of course there were many rumors."

There was another intrusion. Mildred's son-in-law said, "What are you two subversives plotting?"

"We're helping the police solve the Fitch case," Qwilleran informed him.

"Excuse me," Mildred said, "I'm going to get another drink."

Roger said, "I heard something interesting this afternoon, Qwill. A few hours before Nigel shot himself, he dictated letters of resignation from the bank—for David as well as himself. His suicide was evidently premeditated."

"But why would David have to resign?" Qwilleran asked.

Before Roger could think of an answer, Hixie breezed into their midst with her usual breathless enthusiasm. "You'll never believe what happened this afternoon. I was having my hair done at Delphine's, and a huge deer crashed through the front window. He ran right through the shop and out the back window. Broken glass everywhere! And utter panic!"

Qwilleran looked doubtful. "Do you have this story copyrighted, Hixie?"

"It's true! Ask Delphine! The windows are boarded up now, and a sign says, THE BUCK STOPPED HERE. I can't understand why he didn't gore a couple of customers."

Roger said, "Why don't these things happen on our deadline? All we get is a flock of wild turkeys."

Arch Riker was circulating and playing the genial host. Amanda was there, too, drinking bourbon and scowling and complaining. She was wearing a conspicuous diamond ring on her left hand.

Riker, beaming, took Qwilleran aside. "We're taking the plunge, old sock. She may be cantankerous, but I admire her. She ran a successful business for twenty-five years and served on the city council for the last ten. And she doesn't take guff from anyone!"

"She's a remarkable woman," Qwilleran said.

Amanda stepped forward, frowning. "Who called me a remarkable woman?" She demanded belligerently. "You never hear of a remarkable man! He's successful or intelligent or witty, but if a woman is any of those things, she's 'a remarkable woman' like some kind of female freak."

"I apologize," Qwilleran said. "You're absolutely right, Amanda. It's a lazy cliché, and I'm guilty. You're not a remarkable woman. You're successful and intelligent and witty."

"And you're a liar!" she growled. Riker grinned and dragged her away, confiscating her glass of bourbon.

Qwilleran looked around for Mildred. He wanted to hear the rest of her story about Harley's disappearance, but she was in earnest conversation with the stringer from Mooseville, so he went to the buffet. While he was eating his second corned-beef sandwich, he spotted Homer Tibbitt, official historian for the *Something,* leaving the city room. "Homer! Where are you going? The party's only begun!"

"I'm going home. It's 8:30—past my bedtime," said the ninety-four-year-old retired school principal in a high-pitched reedy voice. "My days keep getting shorter. When I'm a hundred, I'll be going to bed before I get up."

"I just wanted to know how well you knew the Fitch family."

"The Fitches? The boys came along after I retired, but I had Nigel in math and history when I was teaching. I knew Nigel's father, too. Cyrus was a character!"

"Is he the one who built the big house in Middle Hummock?"

"Cyrus? Yes indeed! He was a big spender, a big-game hunter, a big collector, a big bootlegger, a big everything."

"Did you say bootlegger?"

"That was something he did on the side," Homer explained plausibly. "The family money came from mining. Cyrus built his house in West Middle Hummock so he could see the big lake from the top of one of the hills. Rumrunners brought the stuff over from Canada and landed on his beach."

"How did he get away with it?"

"Get away with it? One night he didn't get away with it! The sheriff confiscated the whole shipment and poured it on the dump in Squunk Corners. That's why Squunk water is so good for you! . . . Well, it's past my bedtime. Good night."

Qwilleran watched the old man making his exit with vigorous maneuvers of angular arms and legs. Then he caught Mildred alone at the bar. "You were telling me something interesting about Harley when we were interrupted," he said.

"Was I?" She paused to think. "I've had a few drinks . . . Was it about the tarot cards?"

"No, Mildred. It was something about Harley's disappearance after his graduation from Yale."

"Oh! . . . Yes . . . He was traveling . . . That's what the family said . . . Nobody believed it."

"Why didn't they believe it?"

"Well . . . you know . . . people around here . . . gossipy."

"Where did they think he was?"

"Who?"

"Harley."

"Oh! . . . Let's see . . . Ask Roger . . . I've got to sit down."

Qwilleran guided her to a chair and offered to bring her a sandwich and coffee. "How do you like it?"

"What?"

"The coffee."

"Oh! . . . Black."

When he returned with the food, someone told him that Mildred had gone to lie down in the staff lounge, so he ate the sandwich himself and sought out her son-in-law. "Better look after Mildred, chum. She's had too much to drink."

"Where is she?"

"Lying down for a while. She was mentioning Harley's mysterious disappearance a couple of years ago. Know anything about that?"

"Oh, sure. The family said he was traveling, but you know how we are up here. We get bored with the truth and have to invent something. Some people thought he was doing undercover work for the government. I thought he shipped out as a deckhand on a tramp steamer. He liked boats, and that's the kind of offbeat thing he'd do—probably grow a beard, wear a patch over one eye and stomp around like Deadeye Dick."

"He married Belle in Las Vegas. Was he a gambler?"

"I've never heard anything to that effect. If he had one consuming passion, it was sailing. The *Fitch Witch* was a neat boat—twenty-seven feet. He and Gary Pratt used to sail her in races and win trophies."

"Hmmm," Qwilleran said, as suspicion tickled the roots of his moustache. In the last few days— since Harley's murder, to be exact—Koko had taken a sudden interest in things nautical. Several times he had tilted the gunboat picture that hung over the sofa, sometimes violently. And the titles he had started sniffing on the bookshelves were sea stories. First it was *Moby-Dick* and then *Two Years Before the Mast*. Most recently it was *Mutiny on the Bounty*. Qwilleran had explained to himself and others that all cats tilt and sniff; they like to rub a jaw on the sharp corners of picture frames and smell the glue used in bookbinding.

Nevertheless, the nautical connection was a curious coincidence, he thought. And there was another mystifying detail: Koko had been excessively attentive to Harley at the birthday party ... less than twenty-four hours before his murder—almost as if he knew something was going to happen.

SCENE
THIRTEEN

Place: Qwilleran's apartment
Time: Early Monday morning . . . and
       TOO early Tuesday morning
Introducing: PETE PARROTT, a paperhanger from
       Brrr

The phone rang early. It was Francesca. "Is Pete
there yet?" she inquired.

"Who?"

"Pete, the paperhanger. He has the wallcovering
for your studio, and he's going to deliver it this

morning. He can install it today or hold off for a couple of days if you wish."

"The sooner the better," Qwilleran decided. "I'll be needing to use my studio the rest of the week. What's Pete's last name?"

"Parrott. Pete Parrott. He's the one who did your living room when you were out of town. He's the best in the county."

"And the most expensive, I suppose."

"You can afford it," she said, with a flippancy that irritated him. He had always disliked being told what to do with his money, whether he had much or little.

Quickly he started tidying his studio, stuffing papers into desk drawers and removing the debris of bachelor living: two coffee mugs, a tie, waste paper that had missed the basket, a pair of shoes, old newspapers, another coffee mug, a sticky plate, a sweater. He also locked up the cats in their apartment despite their vociferous objections; the busboy had not yet delivered their breakfast.

Then Qwilleran sat down to listen for the doorbell. When it finally rang at 9 A.M., it ushered in Derek Cuttlebrink, delivering chicken liver pâté and two boned froglegs for the howling Siamese. The busboy was in no hurry to return to his place of employment; he wanted to talk about the Theatre Club.

"Too bad they canceled the show just because Harley wasn't in it any more," he said. "I had a pretty good part—the policeman, you know. I even had my cop's uniform fitted. They had to lengthen the pants and sleeves."

"There'll be another play in the fall, and you can audition again," Qwilleran informed him.

"I'm thinking of going back to school in the fall and getting into law enforcement. It's a whole lot better than stacking dirty dishes. Wearing a uniform and riding around in a car all day—that's for me!"

"There's more to police work than wearing a uniform and riding around in a car, Derek, but it would be a good idea to complete your education in any event. By the way, how's our nervous waitress who dropped the tray of cheesecake Friday night?"

"Sally? She's okay. She's getting the hang of the job. But she's going to school in the fall—art school—somewhere Down Below. I wish I had her luck. Her tuition's all paid for—by Mr. Fitch."

"Harley Fitch?" Qwilleran asked with sudden interest.

"No, his father. That's why she was all shook up when he shot himself, although she's already got the money."

In his mind Qwilleran was matching up the suave, sophisticated, handsome banker with the timid, scrawny, stuttering waitress, and trying to imagine some kind of illicit connection.

As if reading his mind, the busboy explained, "Sally's dad is janitor at the bank."

"That's a unique fringe benefit," Qwilleran said. "Perhaps you should consider being a janitor instead of a cop."

At 10 A.M. the paperhanger had still not arrived. . . . Eleven o'clock . . . One o'clock . . . Not until 2:30 did the white commercial van pull up to the carriage house. The driver was a burly young man in white coveralls and white visored cap, with thick blond hair bushing out beneath it. Healthy-looking young men with blond hair were in good supply in this north country.

"Sorry I'm late," he shouted from the bottom of the stairs. "Something came up, and I had to take care of it."

"I wish you had phoned."

"Tell the truth, I didn't even think of it. I was sort of messed up in an emergency."

At least he's honest, Qwilleran thought, and he has an honest face.

"Well, I'd better bring up my gear," he said.

The Siamese, released from their apartment hours before, watched with interest as stepladders, a folding table, buckets, and boxes of tools came up the stairs.

Qwilleran said, "I was out of town when you papered the walls in the living room. You did a first-rate job."

"Yeah, I do good work."

"How long will it take you to do my studio?"

Pete appraised the room with a brief, professional glance. "Not long. Just short strips above the dado, and the plaster's in good shape. A little touch-up with spackle. Sizing dries in nothing flat. And there's no matching. One job I did was all stripes—

even on the ceiling, and they had to be mitered.
Worst thing about it, the whole room was out of
whack. Not a plumb line anywhere! When I finished
I was cock-eyed and walking lopsided."

"Was that Fran Brodie's idea?"

"Yeah, she comes up with some doozies, but this
stuff is easy." The wallcovering was natural tan
cork—thin slices over a rust-colored backing. "Well,
I better get started."

"I'll get the cats out of your way." Koko was in-
specting everything, and Yum Yum was studying the
paperhanger's shoes.

"They don't bother me. They were around the
last time I was here. The big one had his nose in everything I did."

"Koko has a healthy curiosity. Do you mind if I
watch, too?"

Pete wielded yardsticks, shears, knives, brushes,
and rollers with swift assurance.

"You seem to know what you're doing,"
Qwilleran said in admiration. "I'm a confirmed
don't-do-it-yourselfer."

"Been hanging wallpaper since I was fourteen,"
said Pete. "I papered some of the best houses in the
county. Never had a complaint."

"That's a good track record. Did you ever paper
the Fitch mansion in the Hummocks?"

Pete stopped abruptly and laid down his shears.
The expression on his face was difficult to interpret.
"Yeah, I been there, three or four times."

"That was a shocking incident Tuesday night."

"Yeah." Qwilleran noticed that he gulped.

"The police haven't made any arrests, but I understand they're questioning suspects."

"Yeah, they're doing their job." Pete went back to work but not as energetically as before.

"I've never seen the Fitch house," Qwilleran said. "What kind of wallpaper did they like?"

"Raw silk—very plain. I hung a lot of raw silk when Mr. and Mrs. Fitch lived there. Then they moved to Indian Village and wanted the same thing in their condo. They've got some spread!"

"Did you do any work for Harley and his wife when they moved in?"

"Yeah, I did the breakfast room in a crazy pattern with pink elephants. She liked everything jazzy. I did their bedroom, too—all red velvet."

"Would you like a cup of coffee or a cold drink or beer?" Qwilleran asked.

"I wouldn't mind something to drink. Coffee, I guess. Gotta stay sober on this job, even if it isn't all stripes."

Qwilleran thawed some frozen coffee cake in the microwave, pressed buttons on the computerized coffeemaker, and served the repast in the studio, among the ladders and paste buckets. Pete sat on the floor with the plate between his legs. Koko watched him with whiskers curled forward and then applied his nose to the man's shoes and pantlegs with the concentration of a bloodhound on a hot scent.

"Shove him away," said Qwilleran, who was also sitting on the floor with his coffee.

"He's okay. I like animals. This is good coffee cake."

"A friend of mine made it. Iris Cobb. She manages the Goodwinter Farmhouse Museum."

"Yeah, I know her. I did some work for the museum. She's a good cook. I gained about ten pounds before the job was done."

"I wonder if they'll make the Fitch mansion into a museum now," said Qwilleran, edging back into the topic that interested him. "I doubt whether David Fitch wants to live there."

"Yeah, he has that crazy house up on the hill. I can't figure it out, but I guess they like it. They don't go in for wallpaper."

"Harley will be missed at the Theatre Club. He was a good actor and always high-spirited. I never met his wife. What was she like?"

Pete shook his head slowly in silent awe. "She had *everything*!" When Qwilleran registered surprise, he added, "She used to be my girl." There was another gulp.

Qwilleran waited for details, but none was forthcoming, so he said, "You knew her for quite a while?"

"Ever since she went to work for the Fitches—housework, you know. She lived there at the house. That's when I was hanging the raw silk."

"Then you have a personal reason to resent this crime."

"Yeah," he said moodily.

"Why did you let her get away?"

"She didn't want a paperhanger, although I make good money. She wanted a rich man—someone to take her to Vegas and Hawaii and places like that. Well, she got him, but it didn't do her any good."

"A damn shame, Pete."

"Yeah, I really went for that girl." He turned an unabashed face to Qwilleran. "The reason I was late today—the police wanted to ask some questions."

"I'm sure they're questioning everyone who knew Belle. That's the way it's done."

"Yeah, but I guess they thought I had reasons for . . . killing them both."

After the work was finished and Pete had cleared out his ladders and buckets, it was late. Qwilleran had no desire to go out to a restaurant, so he thawed some frozen stew for himself and gave the cats the rest of their chicken liver pâté. Yum Yum nibbled it daintily, but Koko lacked appetite. He prowled the living room nervously, as if a storm might be brewing, although nothing but fine weather was predicted.

"You liked the paperhanger, didn't you?" Qwilleran said to him, "and I think he liked you. He seems like a decent guy. I hope the police don't find a way to pin something on him."

Qwilleran was restless, too. He tuned in and rejected four out-of-county radio stations before settling on WPKX for the local news:

A North Kennebeck motorist driving west on Ittibittiwassee Road narrowly escaped injury when a vehicle behind him, which had been speeding and weaving across the yellow line, passed recklessly, forcing him off the pavement. Following this and other similar incidents, the sheriff's department has announced a new war on drunk driving . . . In other news: Pickax will have posies this summer. Fifty flower boxes on Main Street have been planted with petunias . . . Sports news at this hour: The Pickax Miners beat the Brrr Eskimos in softball tonight, eight to three.

Next Qwilleran tried the out-of-town newspapers, but even the *Daily Fluxion* and *Morning Rampage* failed to capture his attention. He made a cup of coffee and drank only half of it. He wanted to phone Polly but was reluctant to do so; he would have to explain the female architect.

In desperation he pulled *Moby-Dick* off the shelf—a book he had not read since college days—and the first three words grabbed his attention: "Call me Ishmael." Halfway through the first paragraph he settled down with enjoyment. This was the kind of literature that he and Polly used to read aloud during lazy weekends in the country. He was still reading when the 2:30 A.M. freight train sounded its mournful whistle on the north side of town. The Siamese had long since fallen asleep.

And he was still reading when a succession of sirens screamed up Main Street. It sounded like three police cars and two ambulances. A major accident, he told himself. Another drunk driver leaving a bar at closing time. Reluctantly he closed the book and turned out the lights.

Qwilleran slept well that night and dreamed richly. He was embarking on a whaling voyage . . . *seeing the watery part of the world . . . a sailor aloft in the masthead, jumping from spar to spar like a grasshopper.* He was not ready to give up his dreaming when the telephone jolted him awake.

"Qwill, have you heard the news on the radio?" It was Francesca. She and her father had a habit of phoning at an unreasonable hour.

"No," he mumbled. "What time is it?"

"Seven-thirty. There was a car-train accident last night."

"Did you wake me up to tell me that?"

"Wake up, Qwill, and listen to me. Three youths were killed when they rammed their car into the side of a moving freight train."

Qwilleran grunted. "Someone's going to get sued if they don't do something about those dark crossings: no street lights; no red warning lights; no barricades." He was fully awake now. "Kids get a few beers, drive seventy in a forty-five-mile zone, with the radio blasting so they can't hear the train whistle. What does anyone expect?"

"Please, no soliloquy, Qwill. I called to tell you that the victims were three teenagers from Chipmunk, and one of them was Chad Lanspeak!"

Qwilleran was silent as he sorted out his reactions and groped for words.

"I know it's going to be rough on Carol and Larry," Fran went on, "but here's the significance of the accident. Dad says it winds up the Fitch case! The other two kids were the prime suspects!"

Still he said nothing.

"Qwill, have you gone back to sleep?"

"Sorry, Fran, I haven't had my coffee yet. I'll have to think about this for a while. We'll talk about it later."

He replaced the phone gently and touched his moustache almost reverently. It was tingling as it did in moments of intuitive premonition. It was telling him that the car-train accident, no matter what others might say, had no bearing on the investigation of the Fitch murders.

ACT ONE—CURTAIN

INTERMISSION

Following the death of the prime suspects, the concerned citizens of Moose County were noticeably relieved. It was over! Everyone knew the homicide detective had returned to his headquarters in the state capital.

Furthermore, it was June, and they had weddings, graduations, parades, fireworks, picnics, family reunions, and camping trips to think about. Conversation in the coffee shops returned to normal: the weather, fishing conditions off Purple Point, and the selection of a beauty queen for the Fishhook Festival in Mooseville.

Qwilleran alone failed to share their relief. The state detective, he told himself, had left town to catch the real criminals off-guard. It might take time, but someone, somewhere, would be deluded into a false sense of security. Someone would return to the scene of the crime. Someone would talk too freely in a bar. Someone would inform the police.

An uneasy sensation on Qwilleran's upper lip convinced him that the final curtain had not fallen on the Fitch murder case.

Act Two

SCENE ONE

Place: Qwilleran's apartment; later,
       Stephanie's restaurant

Time: Late afternoon on the day follow-
      ing the car-train accident

Qwilleran sat at the big desk in his cork-lined studio, writing a letter of condolence to Carol and Larry Lanspeak. The Siamese were sitting on his desk in parallel poses—Yum Yum waiting to grab a paper clip and Koko hoping to lick a stamp, a quarter inch of pink tongue protruding in anticipation.

Yum Yum had leaped to the desktop first, arranging her parts in a tall, compact column. She sat on her haunches with forelegs elegantly straight, forepaws close together, tail wrapped around her toes clockwise. Koko followed suit, arranging himself alongside the female in an identical pose, even to the direction of the tail. They were almost like twins, Qwilleran thought, although Koko's strong body and noble head and intelligent eyes and imperious mien gave him a masterful aura that could not be mistaken.

"I feel sorry for the Lanspeaks," he said to the Siamese. His voice sounded rich and mellow, thanks to the cork wallcovering, and the cats liked a rich, mellow, male voice. "I can provide Chad's alibi for the night of the murder, but the Chipmunk stigma will always link him to the killers in the public memory. As the saying goes . . . 'lie down with dogs; get up with fleas.' "

Koko scratched his ear in sympathetic agreement.

"I'm not convinced that the Chipmunk hoodlums killed Harley; there are too many alternatives. I may be beating the drum for an unpopular cause, but I'm going to follow my instincts." He groomed his moustache with his fingertips.

"Harley disappeared for a year after graduation, and no one really knows where he went or what he was doing. He could have been mixed up in almost anything. Just because he was an admirable figure in Pickax, it doesn't follow that he played that role out of town. He was a versatile actor, and he liked to play against type. That Boris Karloff bit he was rehearsing was his kind of number."

Koko blinked in apparent acquiescence; Yum Yum maintained her wide-eyed, baffled, blue stare.

"His year of sowing wild oats, if that's what it was, could have led to blackmail. He could have made enemies. He might have experimented with drugs and become involved with a drug ring. And a sexual escapade with some questionable character, male or female, is not beyond the realm of possibility."

Both cats squeezed their eyes, as if this were heady stuff.

"There's no telling what a young man will do when he cuts loose from his family and hometown. He might have run up gambling debts that he couldn't pay. It was odd that he married Belle in Las Vegas instead of at the Old Stone Church."

Qwilleran was swiveling his chair back and forth as he spoke. Abruptly he stopped and caressed his moustache. "And another possibility! David may have been a silent partner in Harley's adventure. Their grandfather was a bootlegger. Rumrunners from Canada used to land their goods on his beach. Perhaps something else has been landing on that beach. David's house would make a good look-out station."

Both cats now had their eyes closed and were swaying slightly.

"I hope I haven't bored you," he said. "I was just airing a few theories."

He finished writing his note to the Lanspeaks. His messages of sympathy were always beautifully worded; a sincere fellow-feeling had always been one of his assets as a newspaper reporter.

As he was addressing the envelope the telephone rang, and he swiveled to reach it on the table behind him. It was a call from Iris Cobb, manager of the Goodwinter Farmhouse Museum. In her usual cheery voice she asked, "Would you like to come over and see the museum, Mr. Q, before it opens to the public? You could come to dinner, and I'd make pot roast and mashed potatoes and that coconut cake you like."

"Invitation accepted, Mrs. Cobb," he replied promptly, "provided the coconut cake has apricot filling."

She had been his housekeeper when he and the Siamese lived in the big house, and the old formality of address still existed between them. It was always "Mr. Q" and "Mrs. Cobb."

"You could bring Koko and Yum Yum," she suggested. "I miss the little dears, and they'd enjoy prowling around this big place after being cooped up in your apartment."

"Are you sure they'd be welcome in the museum?"

"Oh, yes, they never do any damage."

"Except for an occasional ten thousand–dollar

vase," Qwilleran reminded her. "What day did you have in mind?"

"How about Sunday at six o'clock?"

"We'll be there!" He made a mental note to buy a pink silk scarf at Lanspeak's. Pink was Mrs. Cobb's favorite color. He missed his former house-keeper's cooking. Now, as live-in manager of the museum, she had one wing of the farmhouse as a private apartment—with a large kitchen, she said. The invitation sounded promising.

Qwilleran turned back to his desk and found the desktop strewn with paper clips; the envelope he had been addressing was gone, and two cats were missing. A telltale slurping under the desk led him to Koko and a limp, sticky envelope.

"Okay, you scoundrels," he said as he crawled under the desk. "I consider this antisocial behavior. Shape up, or you'll get no pot roast on Sunday."

When the telephone rang a second time, he stowed the envelope in a drawer. It was five o'clock, and he knew who would be on the line.

"I'm about to leave the studio, Qwill. Do you mind if I drop in to check on Pete's work?"

"Sure, come along, Fran. It's a big success. The cork gives the room a good acoustical quality."

"I knew it would, and your voice sounds perfectly magnificent!" she said. "See you in five minutes." She sounded gayer than usual.

Francesca has been to lunch with a client, Qwilleran thought. To the Siamese he said, "She's coming for a drink, and I don't want anybody grabbing her ankle or stealing her personal property."

Shortly after, the designer turned her own key in the lock downstairs and bounced up to the apartment in high spirits.

"Scotch?" he asked.

"Make it light. I had a lo-o-ong lunch date with a new client. Don Exbridge! I'm doing his new condo in Indian Village."

Qwilleran huffed silently into his moustache. The recently divorced Exbridge was a developer and one of the most eligible catches in town; women melted at his smile.

They carried their drinks into the studio, and Qwilleran sat at his writing desk while Francesca curled up in the big lounge chair where he did his creative thinking and occasionally a little catnapping. She curled up with more abandon than usual, he noted. He said, "The cork walls were a good choice for this room, Fran."

"Thank you. Pete did a great job. He always does."

"Even with mitered stripes?"

"Ah! The Brrr Blabbermouth has been telling tales!" she said with a grimace. "That stripe job was one of my early mistakes. At lunch today Don Exbridge asked for plaid wallcovering in his den, and I vetoed it in a hurry. I told him his whole condo development is out-of-square. He just smiled his enchanting smile. He's very easy to get along with. We're going to Chicago to choose some things for his place."

Qwilleran frowned. "When are you and I flying Down Below to choose my bedroom furnishings?"

Fran reacted with surprise and pleasure. "How about next week? There's a new king-size four-poster I want you to see."

"I don't want anything that looks as if George Washington slept in it," he objected.

"This bed is contemporary. Stainless-steel posts with brass finials. And there are some new case pieces from Germany that you'll like—very neo-Bauhaus. Do you mind if I make the hotel reservations? I know a cozy place near the showroom district—expensive, but it'll go on your bill, and it won't hurt a bit. How about next Wednesday? If we catch the morning shuttle to Minneapolis, we can be in Chicago for lunch."

Qwilleran thought, When Polly finds out about this, it will be the coup de grace.

Fran said, "What else did Big Mouth tell you?"

"About the pink elephants and red velvet that he installed for Harley and Belle. Was that one of your mistakes?"

"NO!" she thundered in her best stage voice. "My boss handled that transaction. Amanda will sell clients anything they want, whether it's bad taste or utterly impractical or illegal. She's corrupt, but I like her."

"Arch Riker is going to marry Amanda."

"I hope he has a sense of humor. He'll need it!"

"Have you heard how the bank will replace Nigel and the boys?"

"Nothing official, but the rumor is that two women officers will be elevated to VP, and a new president will come in from Down Below. I hope he'll need an interior designer."

"Where were you when you heard about the suicide?" he asked.

"At the hairdresser's. Everyone cried. People really loved Nigel. He was so suave and good-looking and charming!"

"I was having dinner at the Old Stone Mill," Qwilleran said, "and one of the waitresses dropped a tray when she heard the news. I presume Nigel was suave, good-looking, charming, and a big tipper."

"Now you're playing the cynical journalist. Bravo!" she said. "Did you hear that Margaret's place on the library board is going to be filled by Don Exbridge?"

Qwilleran grunted in disapproval. Exbridge was the developer who had tried to have the historic courthouse demolished. He said, "Exbridge will convince the city to tear down our historic public library, so he can build a new one for $9.9 million."

"Now you're being vicious as well as cynical!" There was an amused glint in her steely, gray eyes. She liked to goad him. "Don would also like to replace Nigel on the Klingenschoen board of trustees."

"Perfect!" Qwilleran said. "He can manipulate Klingenschoen grants to buy political favors, like rezoning, tax abatement, sewers, and other benefits for his private enterprises . . . May I freshen your drink? Then we'll go to Stephanie's for dinner." Mischievously he added, "I heard some curious news last week. I heard that Harley disappeared for a year after finishing college." He knew it would ruffle her.

"He didn't *disappear*! He traveled for a year. For centuries young men have taken the grand tour before settling down. Nothing unusual about that!" She was on the defensive now.

"The consensus is that he did something unconventional during his year of freedom."

"Stupid gossip!" she said testily.

"Did he travel by plane, motorcycle, or camel?"

"Frankly, I never thought it important to ask."

"Did he discuss his itinerary?"

"The Fitches would consider it tacky to bore people with their travels. And he didn't bring home any color slides or French postcards or plastic replicas of the Taj Mahal. . . . What am I getting? The third degree?"

"Sorry . . . How's David? Have you seen him, or talked with him?"

"I talk to Jill on the phone every day," Fran said, relaxing after her brief flurry of annoyance. "She thinks David's on the verge of a breakdown. They're going away for a few weeks—to a quiet place in South America where they spent their honeymoon."

"I suppose David will inherit everything."

"I really don't know." She looked at her watch. "The restaurant stops serving at nine o'clock."

"Okay, let's go . . . as soon as I feed the cats."

"Did you ever find my cigarette lighter?"

"No, but Mr. O'Dell has been alerted to look for it when he cleans."

The Siamese had retired to their apartment and were studiously watching birds from the windowsill. Qwilleran put a plate of tenderloin tips on a placemat in their bathroom, turned on the TV without the audio, and quietly shut the door to their apartment.

On the drive to Stephanie's he said, "Is it true that Harley's grandfather was a bootlegger?" He expected another indignant rebuttal.

"Yes!" she said with delight. "He believed people were going to drink anyway, and if he smuggled in good stuff from Canada, they wouldn't go blind from drinking rotgut. He didn't believe in Prohibition, income tax, or corsets for women."

The draped tables at Stephanie's were placed in the original rooms of the old house, and Qwilleran and his guest were seated in the second parlor. The late sun was still beaming through the stained-glass windows, turning the beveled mirrors and wine glasses into rainbows. Over dinner they discussed the new theater.

Qwilleran said, "They're installing the seats this week. It should be available for rehearsals in August. Do you still want to open with an original revue?"

"Well . . ." Fran said indecisively, "under the circumstances we thought of doing a serious play and asking David to take a role. Something challenging and worthwhile might renew his interest in life. He's so depressed that Jill is afraid he'll follow his father's example."

Qwilleran thought, If David is involved in the situation that led to Harley's execution, he has good reason to be depressed. He could be the next victim. To Fran he said, "Do you have any particular play in mind? Nothing Russian, I hope; it would push him over the brink."

"And nothing too bloody," she said.

"And nothing about two brothers."

A mellifluous voice could be heard in the front parlor, where there were four or five tables for diners. It was a man's voice, talking earnestly, then laughing heartily.

"I recognize that voice," Qwilleran said. "But I can't place it."

Fran peered over his shoulder. "It's Don Exbridge!" she said brightly. "And he's with a woman. I think it's Polly Duncan! They seem to be having a go-o-od time." She looked teasingly smug.

"Aren't you going to send drinks over to their table?"

Qwilleran scowled as a ripple of pleasant laughter came from the front parlor. It was Polly's gentle voice. After that he was impatient with the rest of the dinner: the salad was limp; the hazelnut torte was soggy; the coffee was weak. He was impatient with Fran's conversation. He was impatient to send her on her way, impatient to get home to the sympathetic Siamese. Not once, he recalled, had she mentioned Koko and Yum Yum during the evening; he doubted whether she even knew their names. Not once had she remarked about the new newspaper or commented on the column he was writing. On the whole he was sorry he had agreed to fly Down Below to look at a stainless-steel bed and some neo-Bauhaus chests. There was nothing wrong with his present bedroom furniture. He felt comfortable with it. He had always felt comfortable with Polly, too. He had never felt entirely comfortable with Francesca.

On arriving home he went first to the cats' apartment to check on possible drafts from an open window and to turn off the TV. They were both asleep in one of the baskets, curled up like yin and yang. Then he flicked on the light in the bathroom to see if they had finished their dinner, and to give them fresh water.

The scene was one of havoc! Yum Yum's commode was overturned, and its contents had been flung about the room. A shiny object, half-buried in a damp mound of kitty gravel, proved to be a silver cigarette lighter.

Something, Qwilleran thought, is radically wrong with that cat! She used to be so fastidious! Tomorrow she goes to the doctor!

Place: Qwilleran's apartment
Time: The morning after Yum Yum's
demonstration
Featuring: AMANDA GOODWINTER

As he dialed the animal clinic to make an appointment for Yum Yum, Qwilleran thought, It was stupid of me to buy her a plastic dishpan; she wanted equal rights! She wanted an oval roasting pan like Koko's.

He was explaining the situation to the receptionist at the clinic when the doorbell rang—three insistent rings. Only one person in Pickax rang doorbells like that.

Amanda Goodwinter clomped up the stairway complaining about the weather, the truckdrivers on the construction site, and the design of the stairs— too steep and too narrow. The love of a good newspaperman had done nothing to improve her disposition or her appearance. Wisps of gray hair made a spiky fringe under the brim of her battered golf hat, and her washed-out khaki suit looked unfitted and unpressed.

"I came to see if my free-loading assistant is making any progress," she said, "or is she just taking long lunch hours with clients?"

"I think you'll be pleased with what she's done," Qwilleran said.

"I'm never pleased with anything, and you know it!" She trudged around the apartment, glaring at the wallcoverings and built-ins and accessories, mumbling and grumbling to herself.

"Francesca plans to design some enclosures for the radiators," he said.

"Planning it is one thing; doing it is another." She straightened the gunboat picture, which Koko had tilted again. "Where did you get this print?"

"From an antique shop in Mooseville that's run by an old sea captain."

"It's run by an old flimflam artist! He never went farther than the end of the Mooseville pier! There are ten copies of this picture floating around the county—all cheap reproductions, not original prints.

The only original is in the Fitch mansion, and it's there because I sold it to Nigel as a birthday present for Harley. Never did pay me for it!"

"I understand you helped the family with their decorating," Qwilleran said.

"There's nothing anyone could do with that place except burn it down. Did you ever see the junk old Cyrus collected? They're supposed to be treasures. Half of it's fake!"

"The paperhanger told me they have some pretty wild wallpapers."

"Arrgh! That tramp Harley married! I gave her what she wanted, but I made sure it's peelable wallpaper. I hope somebody has the sense to peel it off! They should go in with a backhoe and shovel out all the crap! All those mangy stuffed animals and molting birds and phony antiques! Don't know what they'll do with the old mausoleum now. Might as well dynamite the whole thing and build condos."

"Would you like to sit down, Amanda, and have a cup of coffee?"

"No time for coffee! No time to sit down!" She was still tramping back and forth like a nervous lioness. "Besides, that stuff you call coffee tastes like varnish remover."

"With the Fitch family virtually wiped out," Qwilleran said, "this community has suffered a great loss."

"Don't waste any tears over that crew! They weren't as perfect as the lunkheads around here like to think."

"But they were civic leaders—active in all the service clubs and all the fund-raising drives. They served the community unselfishly." He was aware that he was baiting her.

"I'll tell you what they were up to, mister; they were polishing their egos! Fund-raising—pooh! Just try to get any money out of their own pocketbooks, and it was a different story. And were they ever slow to pay their bills! I should've charged 'em the same interest the bank charges!"

Qwilleran persisted. "The daughter of the janitor at the bank is going to art school, and Nigel Fitch personally paid her tuition."

"The Stebbins girl? Hah! Why not? Nigel's her natural father! Stebbins has been blackmailing him for years! . . . Well, I can't stay here all day, completing your education." She started down the stairs. Halfway down she said, "I hear you're going to Chicago with my assistant."

"We have to choose some furniture for my bedroom," Qwilleran said. "By the way, when's the wedding?"

"What wedding?" she shouted and slammed the front door.

SCENE THREE

Place: The Black Bear Café
Time: Evening of the same day
Introducing: GARY PRATT, barkeeper, sailor, and
friend of Harley Fitch

Qwilleran had three reasons for driving to the Hotel Booze in Brrr on Thursday evening. He had a yen for one of their no-holds-barred hamburgers. Also, he wanted another look at the black bear that had scared the wits out of him at his birthday party. But mostly, he wanted to talk with Gary Pratt, the barkeeper who had sailed with Harley on the *Fitch Witch*.

He telephoned Mildred Hanstable, who lived a few miles west of Brrr, to ask if she would like to meet him for a boozeburger. She would, indeed! Women never declined Qwilleran's invitations.

She said, "I'd like to see what Gary's done to the hotel since his father let him take over."

"I hope he hasn't cleaned it up too much," Qwilleran said. "And I hope Thumbprint Thelma hasn't quit. I wonder if they still set ant traps under all the tables."

The Hotel Booze was built on a sandhill overlooking the lakeside town of Brrr. It was an old stone inn dating back to pioneer days when there were no frills, no room service, no bathrooms, and (on the third floor) no beds. In its "Publick Room" miners and sailors and lumberjacks gathered on Saturday nights to drink red-eye, eat slumgullion, gamble away their pay, and kill each other. From those turbulent days until the present the hotel had been distinguished by its rooftop sign. Letters six feet high spelled out the message: BOOZE ROOMS FOOD.

Most of Moose County considered the Hotel Booze a dump. Nevertheless, everyone went there for the world's best hamburgers and homemade pie.

Qwilleran and his guest met in the parking lot and walked together into the Publick Room, now renamed the Black Bear Café. At the entrance the bear himself stood on his hind legs, greeting customers with outstretched paws and bared fangs.

"The room looks lighter than before," Mildred observed.

Qwilleran thought it was because they had washed the walls for the first time in fifty years. "And they repaired the torn linoleum," he said, looking at the silvery strips of duct tape crisscrossing the floor. "I wonder if they reglued the furniture."

He and Mildred seated themselves cautiously on wooden chairs at a battered, wooden table. A sign on the empty napkin dispenser read: PAPER NAPKINS ON REQUEST, 5¢.

Behind the bar was a hefty man with a sailor's tan, an unruly head of black hair and a bushy black beard, lumbering back and forth with heavy grace, swinging his shoulders and hairy arms as he filled drink orders calmly and efficiently.

Mildred said, "Gary's getting to look rather formidable. I'm glad he's taking an interest in the business. He didn't show much promise in school, but he made it through two years of college and stayed out of trouble, and now that his father is ill he seems to be showing some initiative."

Towering boozeburgers were served by a young waitress in a miniskirt. "Where's Thelma?" Qwilleran asked, remembering the former waitress who ambled out in a faded housedress and bedroom slippers.

"She retired."

Thelma had always served the toppling burgers with her thumb on top of the bun; now they were skewered with cocktail picks.

Mildred said, "I hope I didn't disgrace myself at the office party Saturday night."

"They were pouring the drinks too stiff. I had three corned-beef sandwiches and two dill pickles and regretted it later."

"I liked your column on Edd Smith, Qwill. It's about time he had some recognition."

"He's amazingly well-read. He quotes Cicero and Noel Coward and Churchill as easily as others quote the stars in a TV serial. But how does he make a living in that low-key operation? Does he have a sideline? Extortion? Counterfeiting?"

"I hope you're only trying to be funny, Qwill. Edd is an honest, sweet-natured, pathetic little man . . ."

". . . who keeps a deadly weapon next to his toothbrush."

"Well, I have a handgun, too. After all, I live alone, and in summer all those batty tourists come up here."

"Speaking of handguns," he said, "I was having dinner at the Old Stone Mill when we heard that Nigel had shot himself, and one of the waitresses reacted very emotionally. I hear she's an art student. Her name is Sally."

"Yes, Sally Stebbins. She received a scholarship from the Fitch family, and I imagine she felt the loss deeply."

"How did she rate a scholarship? Is she a good artist?"

"She shows promise," Mildred said. "Fortunately her father works at the bank, and Nigel has always taken a paternal interest in employees and their families." She regarded him sharply. "I hope you're not resurrecting the old gossip."

"Is it worth resurrecting?"

"Well, I may as well tell you, because you'll dig until you find out anyway. There was a rumor that Nigel was Sally's real father, but it was a despicable lie. Nigel's integrity has always been beyond reproach. He and Margaret were simply wonderful people."

Qwilleran gazed at her intently and fingered his moustache. Did she believe what she was saying? Was it the truth? What could anyone believe in this northern backwoods where gossip was the major industry? He asked her, "What was your reaction to the car-train accident?"

Mildred shook her head sadly. "I regret the loss of human life, but it seems like poetic justice if they're the ones who killed Harley and Belle. Roger says the police haven't found the jewels. Did you know some valuable pieces are missing? They're hushing it up, but Roger has a friend in the sheriff's office."

The waitress in the miniskirt announced the pie of the day: strawberry. It proved to be made with whole berries and real whipped cream, and Qwilleran and his guest devoured it in enraptured silence. Then Mildred inquired about the Siamese.

"Koko's okay," he said, "but I had to take Yum Yum to the vet. I phoned him about her problem, and he told me to bring her in with a urine sample."

"Interesting! How did you manage that?"

"Not with a paper cup! I had to buy a special kit—a minuscule sponge and some tiny tweezers—and then sit in the cats' apartment for five hours, waiting for Yum Yum to cooperate. When the mission was finally accomplished I took her to the clinic with the sponge in a plastic bag the size of a Ritz cracker. I felt like a fool!"

"How did Yum Yum feel?"

"Hell hath no fury like a female Siamese who hates the vet. As soon as she saw the cold, steel table, the fur began to fly. Cat hairs everywhere! Like a snowstorm! She was probed and poked and squeezed and stuck with a thermometer. The vet was murmuring soothing words, and she was howling and struggling and snapping her jaws like a crocodile."

"Did he find anything wrong?"

"He said it's all psychological. She's objecting to something in her life-style or environment, and I don't think it's the new wallpaper. In my opinion she's jealous of the interior designer."

"Really?" said Mildred. "How does Koko react to the designer?"

"He ignores her. He's too busy sniffing glue."

Over the coffee Mildred said, "Confidentially, Qwill, is Roger doing all right at the paper?"

"He's doing fine. He has a history teacher's nose for accurate facts, and he writes well."

"I worried about his giving up a good teaching position—with a new baby in the family and Sharon not working. But I guess his generation is more daring than ours."

"Speak for yourself, Mildred. I, for one, like to make daring decisions."

"Have you decided to get married again?" she asked hopefully.

"Not *that* daring!"

After she said good night, adding that she wanted to be home before dark, Qwilleran moved to a stool at the bar. He had been there before, and Gary Pratt remembered his drink: Squunk water with a dash of bitters and a slice of lemon.

"How do you explain your policy on paper napkins?" Qwilleran asked him.

"Everything costs money," Gary said in a surprisingly high-pitched voice. "The bank stopped giving me free checks, and the gas station stopped giving me free air. Why should I give them free napkins?"

"I admire your logic, Gary."

"The thing of it is, when I kept the dispensers full of napkins they were always disappearing. My customers used them to blow their nose, clean their windshield, and God knows what else."

"You've convinced me! Here's my nickel. I'll take a napkin," Qwilleran said. He nodded toward the mounted bear at the entrance. "I see you've employed a new bouncer."

"That's Wally Toddwhistle's work. He's the best in the business."

"I'm interviewing Wally tomorrow for the paper."

"Mention the Black Bear Café, will you?" Gary

said. "Give us a plug. Tell them the hotel is over a hundred years old, with the original bar." He ran a towel over its scarred surface with affection. "My old man let the place run down, but I'm fixing it up. Not too fancy, you know. We get a lot of boaters, and they like the beat-up look."

Qwilleran glanced around the room and noticed boaters with striped jerseys and tanned faces, farmers in feed caps, men and women in business suits, and elderly folks with white hair and hearing aids. All were eating boozeburgers and strawberry pie and looking happy—with one exception. A sandy-haired man seated a few stools down the bar was drinking alone, hunched over his beer in a posture of dejection. Qwilleran noticed he was wearing expensive-looking casual clothes and a star sapphire on his little finger.

"How long has the big sign been on the roof?" Qwilleran asked Gary.

"Since 1900, as far as I can trace it. It's visible from the lake. In fact, if sailors line up the steeple of the Brrr church with the Z in 'Booze,' it'll guide 'em straight through the channel west of the breakwall." He filled an order for the barmaid and returned to Qwilleran. "Some folks in town object to 'Booze' in such big letters, but, the way I see it, it's a friendly word. Boozing means sitting around, talking and taking it easy while you sip a drink. It goes back to the fourteenth century, only it was spelled b-o-u-s-e in those days. I looked it up."

Gary had professional aplomb. His black eyes

roamed about the café constantly, all the while he talked and worked. He would pour a shot of whiskey, greet a newcomer, ring up a tab, nudge a boisterous customer on the shoulder, wipe the bar, mix a tray of martinis for the barmaid, draw a pitcher of beer, caution a masher, wipe the bar again.

"The thing of it is," he explained to Qwilleran, "Brrr is a harbor of refuge for boats, the only one this side of the lake. I want the café to be a place where everyone can come and feel comfortable and at home."

"I understand you're a sailor yourself."

"I've got a catamaran. She's been in a few races. I used to sail with Harley Fitch, but those days are over. Too bad! Harley and David used to come in here a lot, and we'd talk boats. Not David so much; he's a golf nut. Shoots in the low seventies. Ever see Harley's model ships?"

"No, but I've heard about them. Pretty good, I guess."

"I tried to buy one of his America's Cup racers for the café, but he wouldn't part with it. The thing of it is, he was getting kind of funny toward the end."

"How do you mean—funny?"

"There was his marriage, for one thing. That was all wrong. But there were other things. When he went to work for the bank, I tried to get a loan to improve this place. If I'm gonna rent the rooms, I gotta put in an elevator and bring everything up to code. All that takes money—a lot of money. His father was president of the bank, you know, and I thought we were good friends and could work out a deal."

The barkeeper moved away to refill a glass. When he returned, Qwilleran said, "Did the loan go through?"

Gary shook his shaggy black hair. "No dice. I was really teed off about that, and I gave it to him straight from the shoulder. We had a row, and he never came in here again . . . I didn't care. The thing of it is, he was never the same after he came home."

"Came home from where?" Qwilleran asked with a display of innocence. "From college?"

"No, he was, uh . . . David came home and went into the bank with his father, but Harley spent a year in the east before he came home."

Qwilleran ordered another Squunk water and then leisurely inquired what Harley was doing in the east.

Gary's black eyes roamed the room. "The family didn't want anybody to know, and people made a lot of wild guesses, but Harley told me the truth. When you get out there on the lake with a blue sky full of sail and only the whisper of a breeze, it's easy to talk. It's like going to a shrink. That was before things turned sour between us, you know. I promised to keep mum about it."

Qwilleran sipped his drink and glanced idly at the backbar with its nineteenth-century carvings and turnings and beveled mirrors.

Gary said, "I didn't say anything about it when

the police were here. After the murder they were talking to everybody that knew him."

Qwilleran said, "Do you think Harley's secret mission may have had some bearing on the murder?"

Gary shrugged. "Who knows? I'm no detective."

"Personally," Qwilleran said in his best confidential manner, "I'm not convinced the Chipmunk kids were responsible for the crime, and I think we should do everything we can to bring the real criminals to justice. At the moment I'm wondering if Harley made enemies during his year away from home. Did he get mixed up in gambling or drugs?"

"Nothing like that," said the barkeeper. "I could tell you, I suppose. It doesn't make any difference now that he's dead, and his folks are dead."

Qwilleran's mournfully sympathetic eyes were fixed on Gary's shifting black ones.

Gary said, "But I'd be crazy to tell a reporter. I know you're writing for the paper. Are you digging up some dirt about the Fitches?"

"Nothing of the kind! I'm concerned because Carol and Larry Lanspeak are good people, and I hate to see their boy falsely linked to the murder."

Gary was silent and thoughtful as he wiped the bar for the twentieth time. He glanced around the room and lowered his voice. "Harley's folks said he was traveling out of the country. The thing of it is . . . he was doing time."

"He was in jail?"

"In prison—somewhere in the east."

"On what charge?"

"Criminal negligence. Car accident. A girl was killed."

"Did Harley tell you this?" Qwilleran asked.

"We were still friendly then, and he wanted to get it off his chest, I guess. It's tough living with a secret in a tight little place like Moose County."

"And there's always the chance that someone from outside will come into town and reveal it."

"Or some skunk of a newspaper reporter will dig it up and make trouble."

"Please!" Qwilleran protested.

"Maybe I shouldn't have told you."

"In the first place, I don't consider myself a skunk of a reporter, Gary, and in the second place, my only concern is to find a clue to the identity of the killer—or killers."

"Can you make anything out of it—the way it stands now?"

"One possibility comes immediately to mind," Qwilleran said. "The victim's family may have thought Harley paid too small a price for his negligence. They obviously knew he was affluent. So they came gunning for him. An eye for an eye . . . and a little jewel robbery on the side. I understand the Fitch jewels are missing."

"If you talk to anybody about it," Gary said, "don't get me involved. I can't afford to stick my neck out. When you have a bar license, you know, you have to walk on eggs."

"Don't worry," Qwilleran said. "I protect my

sources. Actually, I suspect the police already know about Harley's prison term, but I'm glad you told me . . . It is a far, far better thing that you do than you have ever done—to paraphrase a favorite author of mine."

"That's from an old movie," Gary said.

"Ronald Colman said it. Dickens wrote it."

The barkeeper became affable. "Do you sail?"

"You're looking at a one hundred-percent landlubber."

"Any time you want to go out, let me know. There's nothing like sailing."

"Thanks for the invitation. What's my tab? I've got to be going."

"On the house."

"Thanks again." Qwilleran slid off the bar stool and then turned back to the bar. "Did anyone ever tell you, Gary, that you look like a pirate?"

The barkeeper grinned. "The thing of it is, I'm descended from one. Ever hear of Pratt the Pirate? Operated in the Great Lakes in the 1800s. He was hanged."

On the way out of the café Qwilleran gave the black bear a formal salute. Then he sauntered out of the hotel, pleased with the information he had gleaned. He ambled to the parking lot, unaware that he was being followed. As he unlocked the car door he was startled by the shadow of someone behind him. He turned quickly.

The man standing there was the blond barfly with

the star sapphire and the melancholy mood. "Remember me?" he asked sullenly.

"Pete? Is that you? You startled me."

"Wanted to talk to you," the paperhanger said.

"Sure." When Pete made no move to begin, Qwilleran said, "Your car or mine?"

"I walked. I live near here."

"Okay. Hop in." They settled in the front seat, Pete slumped in an attitude of despair. "What's bothering you, fella?"

"Can't get her off my mind."

"Belle?"

Pete nodded.

"It will take time to get over that horrible incident," Qwilleran said, going into the sympathy routine that he did so well. "I understand your grief, and it's healthy to grieve. It's something you have to muddle through, one day at a time, in order to go on living." He was in good form, he thought, and he felt genuinely sorry for this hulk of a man whose tears were beginning to trickle down his face.

"I lost her twice," Pete said. "Once when he stole her away from me . . . and once when he got her murdered. I always thought she'd come back to me some day, but now . . ."

"The shooting wasn't Harley's fault," Qwilleran reminded him. "Both of them lost their lives."

"Three of them," Pete said.

"Three?"

"The baby."

"That's right. I had almost forgotten that Belle was pregnant."

"It was my kid."

Qwilleran was not sure he had heard correctly.

"That was my kid!" Pete repeated in a loud and angry voice.

"Are you telling me that you were sleeping with Belle after her marriage?"

"She came to me," Pete said with a glimmer of pride. "She said he wasn't doing her any good. She said he couldn't do anything."

Qwilleran was silent. His fund of sympathetic sentiments was not equipped for this particular situation.

"I'd do anything to get the killer," said Pete, snapping out of his dejected mood. "I heard you talking in the bar. *I'd do anything to get him!*"

"Then tell me anything you know—anyone you suspect. Frankly, it might save your hide. You're in a sticky situation. Were you doing any work for Harley and Belle at the time of the murder?"

"Papering a bedroom for a nursery."

"Were you working that day?"

"Just finishing up."

"What time did you leave?"

"About five."

"Was Harley there?"

"She said he was out sailing. He did a lot of sailing. He had a boat berthed at Brrr—a twenty-seven-footer."

"Who was with him? Do you know?"

Pete shook his head. "He used to go out with Gary from the Booze. Then Gary got his own boat, and Harley stopped coming into the bar. I saw him at the Shipwreck Tavern a coupla times, though— with a woman."

Qwilleran remembered Mildred's tarot cards. *A deceitful woman involved!* "Do you know who she was?"

Pete shrugged. "I didn't pay that much attention."

"Okay, Pete. I want you to think about this. Think hard! Think like a cop. And if you come up with anything that might throw suspicion in any direction, you know how to reach me. Now I'll drive you home."

Qwilleran dropped the paperhanger at a terrace apartment halfway down the hill and waited until the man was indoors. Then he drove home, wondering how much of the story was true.

That Pete hated Harley for stealing his girl was undoubtedly a fact. That Pete hated Belle for deserting him was a possibility. That Harley proved to be impotent and that Belle turned to Pete for solace might be a wild fantasy in the mind of a disappointed lover. In that case, Pete was a logical suspect. He had the motive and the opportunity, and in Moose County everyone had the means. Belle was the first to be killed, according to the medical examiner. She and Pete might have argued in the bedroom, and he might have shot her in a fit of passion. But he was cool enough to wreck the room and make it look like burglary. One would suppose that he was about to leave the house with the smoking gun and a few jewels in the pocket of his white coveralls, when Harley returned from sailing. They met in the entrance hall. Perhaps they had a few words about the fine weather for sailing and the difficulty of hanging wallpaper in an old house with walls out-of-square. Then Pete presented his bill and Harley wrote him a check. Perhaps Harley offered him a drink, and they sat in the kitchen and had a beer, after which they said "Seeya next time" and Pete pulled out his gun and eliminated Harley.

There was a flaw in this scenario, Qwilleran realized. Harley would be wearing sailing clothes, and the newspaper account stated that both victims were in their "rehearsal clothes." Also, it was 7:30 when David and Jill approached the mansion and saw a vehicle speeding away on the dirt road, creating a cloud of dust.

More likely, Pete was innocent. He left at five o'clock with his ladders and paste buckets. Harley came home and changed into rehearsal clothes while Belle (who was also in rehearsal clothes for some unexplained reason) put a frozen pizza in the microwave. And then the murder vehicle arrived.

Qwilleran was too tired to figure out how the murderers first killed Belle upstairs and then killed Harley downstairs. Furthermore, there was the possibility that Roger's information from the medical examiner had been distorted by the Pickax grapevine. Slowly and thoughtfully he mounted the stairs to his apartment. At the top of the flight the Siamese were waiting for him, sitting side by side in identical attitudes, tall and regal, their tails curled around their toes—counterclockwise this time. He wondered if the direction had any significance.

Place: The Toddwhistle Taxidermy Studio
in North Kennebeck
Time: The next morning
Introducing: MRS. TODDWHISTLE

In making his appointment with Wally Toddwhistle, Qwilleran asked for directions to the studio.

"You know how to get to North Kennebeck?"
Wally asked. "Well, we're east of Main Street . . . I
mean west. You know Tipsy's restaurant? You go
past that till you get to Tupper Road. I think there's

a street sign, but I'm not sure. If you get to the
school, you've gone too far, and you'll have to turn
around and come back and turn right on Tupper
—or left if you're coming from Pickax. You go quite
a ways down Tupper. There's a shortcut, if you
don't mind a dirt road—not the first dirt road; that
one dead-ends somewhere. There's another dirt
road . . ."

A woman's voice interrupted—a throaty voice
with a great deal of energy behind it. "I'm Wally's
mother. If Wally stuffed owls the way he gives directions, he'd have the feathers on the inside. Got a
pencil? Write this down: Two blocks past Tipsy's
you turn left at the motel and go nine-tenths of a
mile. Turn left again at the Gun Club and we're the
third farmhouse on the right—with a sign out in
front. Pull in the side drive. The studio's out back."

On the way to North Kennebeck Qwilleran visu-
alized Mrs. Toddwhistle as a large woman with
football shoulders, wearing army boots. Wally himself always looked hollow-eyed and undernourished,
but he was a nice kid—and talented.

He allowed an hour for lunch at Tipsy's and even
had time to stop at the Gun Club. The pro shop,
open to the public, was stocked with rifles, shotguns, handguns, shells, scopes and camouflage
clothes. Here and there were mounted pheasants,
ducks, and other game birds.

"Help you, sir?" asked the brisk man in charge.

"Just passing by and stopped for a look,"

Qwilleran said. "Are the birds Wally Toddwhistle's work?"

"Yes, sir! Certainly are!"

"The sign in the window says you teach the use of firearms."

"Certainly do! We don't sell anything to anybody unless they know how to use it. We have classes for children and adults, ladies included. Safety is what we stress, and care of the firearm."

"Do you sell many handguns?"

"Yes, sir! A lot of hunters are using handguns."

"Do you find people buying them for personal protection?"

"Our customers are sportsmen, sir!"

Qwilleran priced the handguns and then went on his way to the taxidermy studio. There was a neat, white farmhouse with lace curtains in the windows and the usual lilac bush by the door and a modern pole barn in the rear. That was the studio.

He was greeted by Mrs. Toddwhistle, with Wally two steps behind her. She was not what he expected, being short and chunky and aggressively pleasant. "Have any trouble finding us, honey?" she asked. "How about a cup of coffee?"

"Later, thanks," he said. "First I'd like to talk to Wally about his work. I saw the stuffed bear at the Hotel Booze last night."

"*Mounted* bear, honey," the woman corrected him in a kindly way. "We don't stuff animals any more, except birds and small mammals. Wally buys or builds a lightweight form and pulls the skin over it like a coat. It's more accurate and not so goshdarned heavy . . . is it, Wally? When they used to stuff animals with excelsior, mice got into them and built nests. My husband was a taxidermist."

"I stand corrected," Qwilleran said. "Be that as it may, the bear looks great! They've got it spotlighted."

"Very bad to have a mounted animal under a spotlight or near heat," she said. "Dries it out . . . doesn't it, Wally? And all the smoking in Gary's bar is going to ruin the pelt. It's beautiful work. A shame to spoil it! Wally didn't charge half enough for that job."

They were in an anteroom with several specimens on display: a bobcat climbing a dead tree, a pheasant in flight, a coyote raising its head to howl. Qwilleran directed a question to the silent taxidermist. "How long have you been doing this work?"

His mother was relentless. "He probably doesn't even remember . . . do you, Wally? He was only a few years old when he started helping his daddy scrape skins. Wally always loved animals—didn't want to hunt them—only preserve them and make them look real. I help him with scraping the meat off the hides, getting the burrs and straw out of the pelts—things like that."

"May I ask you a favor, Mrs. Toddwhistle," Qwilleran began amiably but firmly. "I have a problem. I've never been able to interview two persons at the same time, even though I've been a reporter for twenty-five years. I have an unfortunate block.

Would you mind if I interviewed your son first? After that I'd like to sit down with you and get your story—and have that cup of coffee."

"Sure, honey, I understand. I'll go back to the house. Just give me a buzz on the buzzer when you're done." She bustled from the studio.

When his mother had gone, Wally said, "I haven't heard from Fran. What's the club going to do about a summer show?"

"No summer show, but they plan to do a serious play in September, with rehearsals beginning in August. No doubt you'll be called upon to build the sets, although I don't know who'll design them. Jill is taking David to South America for a few weeks. He's having difficulty adjusting, and she wants to get him away for a while."

"I'm having a hard time accepting it, too," said Wally. "After I heard about the murder, I couldn't work for days; I was so nervous. I'm glad it's all over."

"I'm not convinced of that. New evidence may come to light."

"That's what my mother says. She used to work for the family when Mr. and Mrs. Fitch lived in Grandpa Fitch's house."

"She did?" Qwilleran patted his bristling moustache.

"She cooked for them after my dad died. That's why the murder hit me so hard, and then Mrs. Fitch's stroke and Mr. Fitch's suicide! It was terrible!"

Following this revelation Qwilleran had to struggle to keep his mind on the interview. Wally conducted him into a barnlike area that was a bewildering combination of zoo, furrier's workroom, animal hospital, butcher shop, catacomb, and theater backstage. There were freezers, oil drums, a sewing machine, a wall of bleached animal skulls, a skeletonic long-legged bird. A shaggy, white wolf, not yet fitted with eyes and nose, lay stiffly on its side, its forelegs wrapped in bandages. A brown bear hide was being stretched on a board to make a rug. Fox, skunk, owl, and peacock, were in various stages of dress and undress.

Some of the animals were alive: dogs with wagging tails, a cage of small fluttering birds, a menacing macaw chained to a perch. An orange cat was curled up on a cushion, asleep.

Wally was eager to show and tell: A box of glass eyes included eleven kinds for owls and twenty-three for ducks. "We have to be authentic," he said . . . Plastic teeth, tongues, and palates were for animals being mounted with open mouths. Real teeth, Wally explained, would crack and chip . . . There were ear-liners for deer. He showed how he turned the ears inside out and glued the liners in to stiffen them . . . Also in evidence were animal forms in yellow plastic foam. "They're manikins." Wally said. "They're good because I can sculpture the foam to fit the skin, then coat the manikin with skin paste, pull the skin over it, fit it and adjust it."

Qwilleran said, "You seem to do a lot with adhesives."

"Yes, it takes all kinds—glue, skin paste, and epoxy for things like putting rods in leg bones. I repaired a damaged eyelid by gluing on a piece of string and painting it. You could never tell anything was wrong."

The young man was an artist at reconstructing animals, making them lifelike, bringing out their natural beauty, but Qwilleran was impatient to see his mother again. The buzzer brought her running from the house with coffee and freshly made doughnuts. He edged into the subject of the Fitch family diplomatically.

"I was their cook for seven years," Mrs. Todd-whistle said with pride. "Practically a member of the family."

"I hear the house is a virtual museum."

She rolled her eyes in disapproval. "Grandpa Fitch was a collector. They have tons of stuff all over the house and it all had to be dusted and vacuumed. They even have a man come in to dust the books."

"Why did you leave their employ?"

"Well!" she said with an emphasis that promised a significant story. "The mister and missus moved to a condominium, and they wanted me to stay and cook for Harley and his bride, but I said no way! Belle was the girl who did the dusting, and I certainly wasn't going to take orders from her! All she liked was pizza! She had eyes set close together. Some men think that's sexy, but I say you can't trust anybody with eyes set close together. Harley only married her to spite his parents. He knew it would embarrass them."

Wally said, "Mother, do you think you should talk about that?"

"Why not? They're all dead. Everybody knows it anyway."

Quickly Qwilleran put in, "Why was Harley antagonistic to his family? He seemed like such an agreeable guy."

"Well, you see, Harley was away for a while, and when he came back he found that David had married his girl! Way back in high school it was always Harley and Jill, David and Fran—football games, proms, sailing and everything. It was quite a shock to everybody when Jill married David."

"How did Mr. and Mrs. Fitch feel about it?"

"It was okay with them! They paid for a big wedding. Jill's folks couldn't have afforded such a blast, although they used to have money. Jill comes from good stock."

"I wonder how Fran reacted to the switch."

"I don't know. She didn't come around any more after that. She's a nice girl, with a lot on the ball, but I guess the missus thought she wasn't good enough for David."

Qwilleran combed his moustache with his fingertips. "I didn't know parents dictated their kids' lives any more. It sounds archaic."

"*Money*, honey," said Mrs. Toddwhistle, making a "gimme" gesture with her fingers. "Mister and missus got the boys hooked on high living—boats

and cars and all—then doled out just enough money
so they'd heel and sit up." (One of the dogs trotted
over and sat up, expecting a crumb.) "Yes, they gave
Harley a big sailboat, but it wasn't in his name. The
fancy house that David and Jill live in—it's not
theirs, not a stick of it."

"Wally says you don't subscribe to the Chipmunk
theory about the murder."

"I sure don't! The police ought to talk to that old
boyfriend of Belle's. He was plenty mad when he
got jilted."

"The paperhanger?"

She nodded. "He's a quiet kind of fellow, but still
waters run deep . . . Another doughnut, honey?"

After his third doughnut, Qwilleran thanked them
for the refreshments and the interview and left, saying, "That's a beautiful cat you have. I have a couple of Siamese at home."

"Oh, the orange one?" Mrs. Toddwhistle said. "It
was killed on the highway, and Wally found it and
brought it home. He didn't want to see such a beautiful animal wasted . . . did you, Wally?"

Later in the afternoon Qwilleran sat at his desk in
the studio and tried to organize what he had learned
about the art of taxidermy. There was something
about salting fresh hides to draw out moisture and
tie in the hairs, removing skunk scent with tomato
juice or coffee grounds, freezing skins until they
could be scraped and tanned. Yet, his mind kept returning to Mrs. Toddwhistle's gossip. It threw some

light on the Fitch family and explained Francesca's ruined romance, but it did nothing to further Qwilleran's unofficial investigation. He was hearing conflicting tales from all sides, and he never knew whether his informants were lying or guessing or talking through their hats. Koko, his silent partner in so many previous adventures, seemed to be of no help in pinpointing the truth.

Yum Yum sensed his frustrated mood and sat on the desk with hunched posture and worried eyes. Koko was elsewhere, probably in the living room on the bookshelves.

Qwilleran said to her, "All that cat does is sniff bookbindings and hang around waiting for an envelope to lick. I think your friend Koko is hooked! And it's affecting his senses."

"YOW!" came a loud comment from the living room, and Qwilleran went to track it down. Koko was perched on the back of the sofa, tilting the gunboat picture again.

Qwilleran patted his moustache with sudden comprehension. He would visit the decrepit antique shop in Mooseville, where a bogus sea captain had sold him an "original print" that was only a copy!

SCENE FIVE

Place: The Captain's Mess, an antique
shop in Mooseville

Time: Saturday afternoon

Introducing: CAPTAIN PHLOGG

On Saturday morning Qwilleran took the gun-boat print off the wall and drove to the resort town of Mooseville to follow up Koko's obvious clue.

The evening before, he had phoned Mrs. Cobb at the museum. "What do you know about The Captain's Mess?" he asked. "What do you know about Captain Phlogg?"

"Oh, dear, I hope you didn't buy anything from that old quack," she said.

Qwilleran mumbled something about wanting to write a column on the shop. "Do you know when it's open? There's no listing in the phone book."

"It's open when he feels like it. Saturday afternoon would be the safest."

"See you Sunday," he said. "I have two friends here who are looking forward to your pot roast."

Driving up to the lakeshore he recalled buying the gunboat print from the fraudulent Captain Phlogg. The living room needed a large picture over the sofa, and the two-by-three-foot print was the best he could find for the money. The captain's asking price was twenty-five dollars, but Qwilleran had talked him down to five, including frame.

The shop occupied an old building that was ready to collapse. Both the fire department and the board of health wanted it condemned, but local history buffs declared it a historic site, and the chamber of commerce considered it a tourist attraction. After all, "the worst antique shop in the state" was a distinction of sorts. Collectors came from miles away to visit the crooked little shop run by a crooked little sea captain. Only a town like Mooseville would take pride in an establishment famous for infamy.

Qwilleran arrived at noon on Saturday, hoping for a chance to talk with Captain Phlogg before customers started dropping in, but it was 1:30 before the proprietor approached the premises with unsteady gait and unlocked the door with shaking hand.

The interior reeked of mildew, stale tobacco, and whiskey. A lightbulb dangling from a cord illuminated the collection of dusty, broken, tarnished, water-stained, dirt-encrusted artifacts of marine provenance. Captain Phlogg himself—with his ancient pipe and stubble of beard and battered naval cap—blended into the mess.

Qwilleran showed him the gunboat. "Do you remember this?"

"Nope. Never see'd it afore."

"You sold it to me last summer."

"Nope, it never come from here." The captain had an all-sales-final, no-money-back policy that caused him to disclaim everything he had ever sold.

Qwilleran said, "You sold it to me for five dollars, and I've just found out it's worth hundreds. I thought you'd like to know." Qwilleran enjoyed fighting falsity with falsity.

The captain took the foul-smelling pipe from his mouth. "Lemme look at it . . . Give ye ten for it."

"I wouldn't part with it. It's one of two very rare prints, according to art historians. The other is in the Cyrus Fitch collection. Does that name ring a bell?"

"Never heard of it."

"It's in West Middle Hummock. There was a murder there, week before last. A young sailor named Harley Fitch."

"Never heard of 'im."

"His boat was the *Fitch Witch*."

"Never heard of it."

"He docked around here and hung out at the Shipwreck Tavern."

"Never go there."

"He also built model ships."

"Never heard of 'em."

"Do you know a sailor by the name of Gary Pratt in Brrr?"

"Nope."

"If the model ships come on the market, would you be interested in buying any of them?"

"How much he want?"

"I don't know. He's dead. But the estate might be willing to sell."

"Give 'em ten apiece."

"Is that a firm offer?"

"Take it or leave it be." The captain poured an amber liquid from a flask into a mug and took a swig.

Qwilleran departed with his gunboat picture, grumbling at Koko for giving him a false clue. It never occurred to him that he might have misinterpreted Koko's maneuver.

SCENE
SIX

Place: The Goodwinter Farmhouse
          Museum
Time: Sunday evening
Introducing: IRIS COBB, resident manager of the
          museum

Qwilleran carried a wicker picnic hamper into the
cats' apartment. "All aboard for the Goodwinter
Museum!" he announced. The Siamese, who had
been sunning drowsily on a windowsill, raised their
heads—Koko with anticipation, Yum Yum with ap-
prehension. While the male hopped eagerly into the

hamper, the female—suspecting another visit to the clinic—raced around the room faster than the eye could see. Qwilleran intercepted her in midair, dropped her into the travel coop and closed the lid.

Koko scolded her with macho authority and she hissed with feminist spunk as Qwilleran carried the hamper downstairs to the energy-efficient two-door that served his transportation needs. He also transferred the cats' commodes to the car. They now had a matched pair of oval roasting pans with the handles sawed off to fit the floor of the back seat.

It was a half-hour drive to the museum in North Middle Hummock—out Ittibittiwassee Road and across the Old Plank Bridge, then past the Hanging Tree, where a wealthy man once dangled from a rope. Beyond were prosperous farms and country estates. At the end of a lane lined with maple trees stood the rambling farmhouse, sided with cedar shakes that had long ago weathered to a silvery gray. Qwilleran had visited the house before, when it was occupied by the socially prominent Mrs. Goodwinter. Now the property of the Historical Society, it had been restored to the way it looked one hundred years before.

He drove to the west wing and unloaded the two roasting pans. "Where shall I put these?" he asked without ceremony when his former housekeeper greeted him at the door.

"Oh, you have *two* litterpans now!" she said in surprise.

"A new arrangement—at the request of our Siamese princess."

"Put the pans in the bathroom," she said. "I put a bowl of water in there and a placemat for their dinner. They always loved my pot roast."

"Who didn't?" Qwilleran said over his shoulder as he returned to the car for the hamper. When he opened the lid two necks stretched upward and two heads swiveled to survey the scene. Then the cats emerged cautiously and began a systematic exploration of the resident manager's apartment.

With these important matters concluded, Qwilleran observed the amenities. "You're looking very well," he told his hostess. "Your new responsibilities agree with you."

Her cheerful face, framed by a ruffled pink blouse, was radiant as she peered through the thick lenses of pink-rimmed glasses. "Oh, thank you, Mr. Q!"

"How are your eyes, Mrs. Cobb?"

"No worse, thank heaven." She was a plump and pleasant woman, overly good-hearted, inclined to be sentimental, and brave in the face of the tragedies that had marked her life.

"How do you feel about living out here alone? Do you have a good security system?"

"Oh, yes, I feel very safe. Our only problem, Mr. Q, is mice. We've been thoroughly inspected by the carpenter, mason, plumber, and electrician, and none of them can figure out how the mice are getting in. There's an ultrasonic thing, but it doesn't discourage them. I've set traps with peanut butter and caught three."

"I hope they haven't done any damage to the museum."

"No, but it's something we worry about . . . Would you like to look around the apartment while I wash the salad stuff?"

The focus of her living quarters was the country kitchen, where a round oak table and pressed-back chairs were ready for dinner. (Dinner for three, Qwilleran noticed. Nothing had been said about another guest.) There was a small bedroom with an enormous bed—the kind Lincoln would have liked. And there was a parlor with wing-back chairs in front of the fireplace, a rocker in a sunny window, and a large Pennsylvania German wardrobe that had been in the Klingenschoen mansion at one time. Koko soon discovered the sunny window. He even recognized the wardrobe. Yum Yum stayed in the kitchen, however, where the pot roast was putting forth tantalizing aromas.

Mrs. Cobb said, "I invited Polly Duncan because she helped with research for the museum, but she had a previous engagement. So I called Hixie Rice. She's been advising us on publicity, you know. She had a date to go sailing this afternoon, but she'll be here a little later."

"Hixie is always good company," Qwilleran said, wondering if Polly really had another engagement, or if she was avoiding him.

"You'll never recognize the main part of the

house when you see it," Mrs. Cobb said as she twirled the lettuce in a salad basket. "Remember all that decorator-type wallpaper? When we removed it, we found the original walls had been stenciled, so we did some research on stenciling and got the paperhanger to restore it for us. He was very cooperative. He's a nice young man but down in the dumps because his girl jilted him and married someone wealthy. I told him to forget his old flame and find a girl who'll appreciate him. He's almost thirty; he should get married . . . Now prepare for a surprise!"

She led the way into a section of the house built in the mid-nineteenth century and now restored to the simplicity of pioneer days. Furnishings such as a rope bed, trestle table and pie safe had come from the attics of Moose County residents.

"We want it to look as if our great-great-grandparents still live here," she said. "Can't you just imagine them cooking in the fireplace, reading the evening prayers by candlelight, and taking Saturday night baths in the kitchen?"

The floors sloped; the floorboards were wide; the six-over-six windows had some of the original wavy glass. Mrs. Cobb conducted the tour with professional authority while Qwilleran and Koko tagged along, the latter sniffing invisible spots on the rag rugs and rubbing his back against furniture legs. Yum Yum stayed in the kitchen, guarding the pot roast.

"And now we come to the east wing, added in

1890. We use these rooms to exhibit collections. Here's the Halifax Goodwinter Room with the doctor's collection of lighting devices—from an early rush lamp to an elegant Tiffany lamp in the wisteria pattern—very valuable."

At this remark Qwilleran kept a close watch on Koko, but the cat was not attracted to art glass. He merely rubbed his jaw against the corner of a showcase.

"The Mary Tait MacGregor Room is all textiles. Old Mr. MacGregor gave us his wife's quilts, hooked rugs, jacquard coverlets and so on, all handed down in her family." Koko rolled on a hooked rug done in a distelfink pattern.

The Hasselrich Room featured Moose County documents, which Qwilleran said he would like to study at some future date: land grants, early birth and death certificates, journals of nineteenth-century court proceedings, and ledgers from old general stores, itemizing kerosene at a nickel a gallon and three yards of calico for fifteen cents.

"It breaks my heart to show you the next room, considering what happened," said Mrs. Cobb. "Nigel was president of the Historical Society, and he didn't even live to see it dedicated. That rolltop desk belonged to Cyrus Fitch, and in one of the drawers we found a list of his bootleg customers. Imagine! He was smuggling whiskey during Prohibition! They're all dead now, except Homer Tibbitt."

The cut glass, she said, was donated by Margaret Fitch. A punch bowl, decanters and other serving

ing for a dinner companion. His best friend, Arch Riker, would soon be married and staying home evenings. Most of the women he knew were either too aggressive or too frivolous for his taste. The head librarian was the exception, but he and Polly had played their last scene, and he knew when to bring down the curtain.

He was quiet, lulled into contentment by good food, pleasing environment, and the domestic tranquility of the moment. Mrs. Cobb seemed to sense his mood, and her eyes smiled hopefully. Only the crackling of the fire and Koko's heavy breathing broke the silence. Qwilleran wanted to say something, but for once he was at a loss for words. She was an amenable woman, a comfortable companion. He had only to say "Iris!" and she would say "Oh, Qwill!" with tears streaming down under her thick glasses.

Suddenly there was a rushing, bumping, scrambling, thumping burst of noise from the adjoining room. The man and woman ran to the kitchen. Yum Yum was lying on her side at the base of the gas range with her famous paw extended under the appliance while her tail slapped the floor.

"She's got a mouse!" Qwilleran said. He reached for her and received a snarl in response.

"Leave her alone," Mrs. Cobb said. "She thinks you want to take it away from her."

"That's where the mice are getting in—where the gas lines come into the house," he said. "No wonder she was watching the range all evening. She could hear them."

"Oh, she's a good kitty—a real good kitty!"

"She's smarter than your plumber, Mrs. Cobb."

The tail-thumping slowed and then stopped, and Yum Yum wriggled across the floor, withdrawing her long foreleg with the prize clutched in the sharp claws of her famous right paw. Koko walked into the room and yawned.

Mrs. Cobb looked at him in consternation. "Just like a man!"

Her comment took Qwilleran by surprise. It was out of character for the docile, male-worshipping widow he had known.

"Time to go home," he said, opening the picnic hamper. "It was a wonderful dinner, Mrs. Cobb, and you're to be complimented on the museum. Let me know if there's anything I can do."

With the hamper on the backseat and the two commodes on the floor, Qwilleran tooted a farewell to his hostess on the doorstep and headed the car toward Pickax. He was thankful that Yum Yum had caught her mouse at an auspicious time, saving him from an amorous slip of the tongue. He needed no more women on his trail—least of all, his former housekeeper, who was marriage oriented and tragedy prone. All three of her husbands had died violent deaths.

He drove past the Hanging Tree and across the Old Plank Bridge and then west on Ittibittiwassee Road. There was little traffic. The county had built the road—at great expense—to accommodate Exbridge's condominium development. Most motorists preferred the shorter, more commercial route, however, and the local wags called the new highway Ittibittigraft.

Darkness was falling as he passed the site of the old Buckshot Mine. It was here, he recalled, that he had suffered a serious bicycle accident a year before—a highly questionable accident.

And now . . . it all happened again.

SCENE
SEVEN

Place: A lonely stretch of Ittibittiwassee
Road

Time: Later the same evening

It was late Sunday night, and the traffic on
Ittibittiwassee Road was sparse. Westward bound,
Qwilleran met no cars approaching in the opposite
direction, and he drove with his country brights illu-
minating the yellow lines on the pavement. On either side darkness closed in over the patches of
woods, abandoned mine sites and boulder-studded
pastureland. Now and then a half-moon accentu-

ated the eeriness of the landscape, then retired behind a cloud.

Eventually headlights appeared in Qwilleran's
rearview mirror—country lights excessively bright
until he flicked the mirror to cut the glare. The vehicle was gaining on him. Its pattern was erratic:
swerving into the eastbound lane as if planning to
pass—falling back into line—coming closer—
swerving again to the left. It was a van, and when it
came alongside, it was too close for a prudent driver's peace of mind. Qwilleran edged to the right.
The van crowded closer.

He's drunk, Qwilleran thought, and he steered
close to the shoulder and eased up on the pedal. The
van loomed over the small car. Another inch and it
would bump him off the road. He steered onto the
shoulder . . . Easy! Loose gravel! . . . Skidding! Easy!
Turn into the skid! Baby the brake! . . . And then
the little car hit a boulder and flipped over . . . still
traveling, sliding along the edge of the ditch . . . another jolt, another rollover, twice, before it came to
a shuddering halt in the dry ditch.

There was a moment of stunned disorientation—
pedals and dashboard overhead—seat cushions and
roasting pans everywhere—a shower of kitty gravel.

Why was there no cry from the cats?

Qwilleran unbuckled and climbed out of the door
that had been thrown open by the impact. Then he
crawled back into the dark car and groped for the
hamper. It was lying on the upside-down ceiling,

jammed under a seat cushion, its cover open, the cats gone!

"Koko!" he yelled. "Koko! Yum Yum!"

There was no answer. He thought, They might have taken flight in terror! They might have been flung from the car! In panic he searched the ditch in the immediate vicinity, looking for small light-colored bodies in the darkness. He called again. Utter silence.

Then headlights illuminated the landscape as a car approached from the east, stopping on the shoulder of the road. A man jumped out and ran to the scene. "Are you okay? Anybody hurt?"

"I'm all right, but I've lost my cats. Two of them. They may have been thrown out."

The motorist turned and shouted toward his own car, "Radio the sheriff, hon, and bring the torch!" To Qwilleran he said, "Have you tried calling them? It's heavily wooded along here. They might be hiding."

"They're indoor cats. They never go out. I don't know how they'd react to the accident and unfamiliar surroundings."

"Your car's totaled."

"I don't care about the car. I'm worried about the cats."

"The guy was drunk. I saw him weaving before he crowded you off the road. Seemed like a light-colored van."

The man's wife arrived with a high-powered

flashlight, and Qwilleran started beaming it in the ditch and along the edge of the thicket.

The man said to her, "He had two cats in the car. They escaped or were thrown out."

"They'll be all right," she said. "We had a cat fall from a third-floor window."

"Quiet!" Qwilleran said. "I thought I heard a cry."

The wail came again.

"That's some kind of night bird," the woman said.

"Quiet! . . . while I call them and listen for an answer."

Headlights and a flashing red rooflight appeared in the distance, and a sheriff's car pulled up. The deputy in a brown uniform said, "May I see your operator's license?" He nodded when Qwilleran handed it over. "How did it happen, Mr. Qwilleran?"

The other motorist said, "I saw it all. A drunk driver. Crowded him off the road, and then skipped."

Qwilleran said, "I had two cats in the car, and I can't find them."

The deputy flashed a light around the wreck. "Could be underneath."

The woman said, "We'd better go, honey. The baby-sitter has to leave at 11:30."

"Well, thanks," Qwilleran said. "Here's your flashlight."

"Keep it," the man said. "You can get it back to

me where I work. Smitty's Refrigeration on South Main."

The deputy wrote his report and offered Qwilleran a ride into Pickax.

"I can't leave until I find them."

"You could be out here all night, sir."

"I don't care. After you leave they may come crawling out of the bushes. I've got to be here when they do."

"I'll check back with you on my next round. We're watching this road. I nabbed four DWIs last night."

He left, and Qwilleran resumed his search, calling at intervals and hearing nothing except the night noises of the woods, as some small animal scurried through the underbrush or an owl hooted or a loon cackled his insane laugh.

He extracted the wicker hamper from the wreckage —out of shape but intact. He found the two commodes, also. The roasting pans had fared better than the body of his car. He was grateful for the flashlight.

Another vehicle stopped. "Anybody hurt?" asked the driver, walking over to view the car in the ditch. "Anyone call the police?"

Qwilleran went through the same script. "No one hurt ... The sheriff's been here ... No, thanks, I don't need a ride. I've lost two cats and I have to wait ..."

"Lots of luck," the man said. "There are coyotes

out there and foxes, and an owl can carry off a cat at night."

"Just go on your way, please," Qwilleran said firmly. "When it's quiet, they'll come back."

The car left the scene, but the Siamese did not appear. He snapped off the torch. It was totally dark now—totally dark with the moon behind a cloud. He called again in desperation. "Koko! Yum Yum! Turkey! Turkey! Come and get it!" . . . There was absolute silence.

Once more he combed the ditch with the beam of the flashlight, each time venturing a few yards farther from the wreck. After half an hour of fruitless searching and calling, he groaned as another car pulled up.

"Qwill! Qwill, what are you doing out here?" a woman's voice called out. She left her car and hurried toward him. "Is that your car? What happened? Has anyone called the sheriff? I have a CB." It was Polly Duncan.

"That's not the worst," he said, shining the torch on the wreck. "The cats are lost. They may be hiding in the woods. I'm not leaving here till I find them, dead or alive."

"Oh, Qwill, I'm so sorry. I know how much they mean to you." It was the quiet, soothing voice that had appealed to him during their happier days.

He recounted the entire story.

"But you can't stay here like this all night."

"I'm not leaving," he repeated stubbornly.

"Then I'll stay with you. At least you'll have some

shelter and a place to sit. I'll turn my lights off. Maybe they'll sense your presence and come out . . ."

"If they're still alive," he interrupted. "The sheriff thought they might be pinned under the car. They don't answer when I call their names. Another guy said there are predators out there."

"Don't listen to those alarmists. I'll pull my car farther off the highway, and we'll sit and wait . . . No! I won't listen to any protests. There's a blanket in my trunk. It gets chilly after midnight at this time of year. Put those things in the backseat, Qwill."

He put the commodes and hamper in her car, and then he and Polly settled in the front seat of the car he had given her for Christmas. His gloom was palpable. "I don't mind telling you, Polly, how much those two characters have meant to me. They were my family! Yum Yum was getting more lovable and loving every year. And Koko's intelligence was incredible. I could talk to him like a human, and he seemed to understand every word I said. He even replied in his own way."

"You're speaking in the past tense," Polly rebuked him. "They're still alive and well—somewhere. I have enough faith in Koko to know he'll be able to take care of himself and Yum Yum. Cats are too agile to let themselves get trapped under the car. Flight is their forte, and their best defense."

"But the Siamese have lived a sheltered life. Their world is bounded by carpets, cushions, windowsills, and laps."

"You're not giving them credit for their natural instincts. They might even walk back to Pickax. I read about a cat whose family took him to Oklahoma for the winter, and he walked back to his home in Michigan—over 700 miles."

"But he was accustomed to the outdoors," Qwilleran said.

The sheriff's deputy stopped again, and when he saw Qwilleran's companion, he said, "Do you need any potatoes, Mrs. Duncan?" They both laughed. To Qwilleran he said, "Glad you've got company. I'll keep an eye on you two."

As he drove away Polly said, "I've known Kevin ever since he was in junior high, bringing his homework assignments to the library. His family had a potato farm."

Gradually she talked him out of his pessimistic mood by introducing other subjects. Nevertheless, every ten minutes Qwilleran left the car and walked up and down the roadside, calling . . . calling.

Returning from one disappointing expedition he said to Polly, "You were out late tonight."

"There was a party at Indian Village," she explained. "I usually go home early when I'm driving alone, but I was having such a good time!"

Qwilleran considered that statement in silence. Don Exbridge had a condo in Indian Village.

"The party was given," she went on, "by Mr. and Mrs. Hasselrich, honoring the library board. They're charming hosts."

"I hear Margaret Fitch's place on the board will be filled by Don Exbridge," he said glumly.

"Oh, no! Susan Exbridge is a trustee, and it would hardly be appropriate to have her ex-husband on the board. Where did you hear that?"

"I don't recall," he lied, "but I noticed you were dining with him at Stephanie's, and I assumed you were briefing him on his new duties."

Polly laughed softly. "Wrong! The library needs a new roof, and I was trying to charm him into donating the services of his construction crew. But since you bring up the subject, I saw you dining with a strange woman after you told me you were dining with your architect from Cincinnati."

"That strange woman," Qwilleran said, "happens to be the architect from Cincinnati. You get two black marks for assuming the profession is limited to males."

"Guilty!" she laughed.

The sheriff's car was coming down the highway again, and it stopped on the opposite shoulder. When the deputy stepped out, he was carrying something small and light-colored. He was carrying it with care.

"Oh my God!" Qwilleran said and tumbled out of the car, hurrying across the pavement to meet him.

"Brought you some coffee," the deputy said, handing over a brown paper bag. "From the Dimsdale Diner. Not the best in the world, but it's hot. Temperature's dropping to fifty tonight. Couple of doughnuts, too, but they look kinda stale."

"It's greatly appreciated," Qwilleran said with a sigh of relief as he pulled out his bill clip.

"Put that away," the officer said. "The cook at the diner sent it."

The kindness of Polly and the deputy and the cook at the diner and the motorist with the flashlight did much to relieve Qwilleran's depression, although he still felt a numbness in the pit of his stomach. He wanted to talk about the cats. He said to Polly, "They're always inventing games. Now their hobby is posing like bookends."

"Does Koko still recommend reading material for you?"

"He was pushing biographies until a few days ago. Now he's into sea stories."

"Has he lost interest in Shakespeare?"

"Not entirely. I saw him nuzzling *The Comedy of Errors* and *Two Gentlemen of Verona* the other day."

"Both of those plays involve sea voyages," Polly reminded him.

"I'm sure it's the glue he's sniffing. The subject matter is coincidental. But you have to admit it's uncanny."

"There are more things in Koko's head than are dreamt of in your philosophy," said Polly, taking liberties with one of Qwilleran's favorite quotations.

And so they talked the night away.

Qwilleran said, "Now that I'm dropping out of the Theatre Club, Polly, I'm going to review plays for the paper."

"You'll make a wonderful drama critic."

"It means two passes to every opening night, fifth row, center. I hope you'll be my steady theatre date."

"I'll be happy to accept. You know, Qwill, your columns have been very good. I'm sorry I scolded you about your journalism. I especially liked your profile on Eddington Smith."

"Incidentally, when Edd and I were discussing the Fitch case, I mentioned the possibility of rare-book thieves, and he hemmed and hawed—never would say what was on his mind."

"Well, it's a possibility," she said. "I've heard that Cyrus Fitch owned some pornographic books that certain collectors would commit any crime to possess. They're said to be locked up in a small climate-controlled room along with George Washington's Farewell Address and Gould's *Birds of Great Britain*."

"If Edd lets me go to the mansion to help him dust books, I'll check out the hot stuff," Qwilleran said.

And then she told him something that caused him to wince. "I'm leaving for Chicago Wednesday. A library conference. I'm catching the morning shuttle."

She added a questioning glance. It was customary for him to drive her to the airport, but . . . he and Fran were also leaving on the Wednesday morning shuttle! He thought fast.

"Wait! I think I heard something!" He jumped out of the car and walked a few paces, stalling for time. Here was a ticklish situation! He and Polly were rediscovering their old camaraderie; they had shared the blanket during the chilly hours before dawn; he had hoped for reconciliation. How would she react to a jaunt to Chicago with her rival? As far as he was concerned, it was a business trip to select furniture. Would Polly accept that explanation graciously? Did Fran—with her "cozy hotel"— contemplate it as a business trip? She had made the hotel and travel reservations and would add the charges to his bill—plus an hourly fee for her professional advice, he surmised.

It was awkward at best. One half of his brain ventured to suggest canceling the trip. The other half of his brain sternly maintained his right to schedule a business trip anywhere, at any time, with anyone.

The sky was beginning to lighten in the east, and he walked back to the car. "You stay here. I'm going to look around," he said. "If they holed up for the night, they'll start getting hungry when the sun rises, and they might come crawling out. Watch for them while I go searching."

"Will the glasses help?" Reaching under the seat, Polly handed him the binoculars she used for birding.

The woods that had been a black, incomprehensible mass in the dark of night were becoming defined: evergreens, giant oaks, undergrowth. He walked along the highway to a spot where five, tall elm trees grew in a straight line perpendicular to the road. They were obviously trees that had been planted many years before, possibly to border a path or sideroad to some old farmhouse long since abandoned. He was right. An unused dirt road, almost overrun with weeds, followed the line of trees. If the Siamese had discovered it the night before, they might have sheltered in the remains of the old farmhouse.

A light breeze rustled the lofty branches of the elms and blew strands of spiderweb across his face. Everything was wet with dew. A faint, rosy glow appeared in the east. He found the site of the house, but it was now only a stone foundation tracing a rectangle among the grasses.

He stopped and called their names, but there was no response. He walked on slowly. Now he was reaching the end of the road. Ahead were the withered trees of a long-neglected orchard, rising in grotesque shapes from a field of weeds. He scanned the orchard with the binoculars, and his heart leaped as he saw a bundle of something on the branch of an old apple tree. He walked closer. The sky was brightening. Yes! The indistinct bundle was a pair of Siamese cats, looking like bookends. They were peering down at the ground, wriggling their haunches as if preparing to leap.

He lowered the field of vision to the base of the tree and his eyes picked up something else, half concealed in the grasses. A ghastly thought flashed through his mind. Could it be a trap? A trap like those that Chad Lanspeak used for foxes? In horror he edged closer. No! It was not a trap. It moved. It was some kind of animal! It was looking up in the tree! The cats were wriggling, ready to jump down!

"Koko!" he yelled. "No! Stay there!"

Both cats jumped, and Qwilleran fled back to the car, shouting to Polly, "I need your car! Radio the sheriff to pick you up! I've found the cats. I'm taking them to the vet!"

"Are they hurt?" she asked in alarm.

"They've had a run-in with a skunk! Don't worry . . . I'll buy you a new car."

SCENE EIGHT

Place: Qwilleran's apartment
Time: The day after the accident on
Ittibittiwassee Road

Qwilleran's car had been towed to the automobile graveyard; Polly's cranberry-red car was at Gippel's garage, being deodorized; the Siamese were spending a few hours at the animal clinic for the same purpose.

In his apartment Qwilleran paced the floor, chilled by the realization that they might have been lost forever in the wilderness. They might have suffered a horrible death, and he would never have known their fate. The sheriff's helicopter and the mounted posse and the Boy Scout troop would hardly go searching for those two small bodies. He shuddered with remorse.

It was all my fault, he kept telling himself. He was convinced that it was no drunk driver who ran him off the road; it was someone who was out to get him because he had been asking questions about the murderer of Harley and Belle. Why did he have this compulsion to solve criminal cases? He was a journalist, not an investigator. Yet, he was aware, few journalists accepted their limitations. The profession was teeming with political advisors, economic savants, critics and connoisseurs.

No more amateur sleuthing! he promised himself. From now on he would leave criminal investigation to the police. No matter how strong his hunches, no matter how provocative the tingling sensation in the roots of his moustache, he would play it safe. He would interview hobbyists and sheep farmers and old folks in nursing homes, write a chatty column for *The Moose County Something*, read *Moby-Dick* aloud to the Siamese, take long walks, eat right, live the safe life.

And then the telephone rang. It was Eddington Smith calling. "I talked to the lawyer, and he said I should check the books against the inventory. You said you'd like to help with the dusting. Do you want to come with me tomorrow?"

Qwilleran hesitated for only the fraction of a moment. What harm would there be in visiting the Fitch library? Everyone said it was an interesting house—virtually a museum.

"You'll have to pick me up," he told the bookseller. "I've wrecked my car." When he turned away from the phone he was finger-combing his moustache in anticipation.

After lunch Mr. O'Dell drove to the clinic in his pickup and brought home two bathed, deodorized, perfumed and sullenly silent Siamese in a cardboard carton punched with airholes. When the box was opened they climbed out without a glance one way or the other and stole away to their apartment, where they went to sleep.

"A pity it is," said Mr. O'Dell. "The good souls at the clinic were after doin' their best, but sure an' the smell will come back again if the weather turns muggy. It'll just have to wear off, I'm thinkin' . . . And is there anythin' I can do for you or the little ones, since you're lackin' a car?"

"I'd appreciate it," Qwilleran said, "if you'd go to the hardware store and buy a picnic hamper like the old one that was smashed."

The Siamese slept the sleep that follows a horrendous experience. Every half hour Qwilleran went to their apartment and watched their furry sides pulsating. Their paws would twitch violently as if they were having nightmares. Were they fighting battles? Running for their lives? Being tortured at the animal clinic?

Earlier Fran Brodie had telephoned. "I hear you rolled over last night, Qwill."

"Where did you hear that?"

"On the radio. They said you weren't seriously hurt, though. How are you?"

"Fine, except when I breathe. I get a stitch in my side."

"Now you'll have to drive that limousine you inherited." She enjoyed teasing him about the pretentious vehicle in his garage.

"I got rid of it. It was a gas guzzler and hard to park, and it looked like a hearse. It was only standing in the garage, losing its charge and drying out its tires, while I was paying insurance and registration fees every year. I sold it to the funeral home."

"In that case," Fran said, "we can drive my car to the airport Wednesday. We should leave about eight A.M. to catch the shuttle to Chicago. I made the hotel reservations for four nights. You'll love the place. Quiet, good restaurant—and that's not all!"

Qwilleran hung up the phone with misgivings. Burdened with other concerns, he had given no thought to this particular dilemma.

Shortly after that, Polly had called to inquire about the cats.

He said, "It's been a blow to their pride. They usually carry their tails proudly, but today they're at half-mast. Gippel is working on your car, Polly, but I want you to have a new one, and I'll drive the red job."

"No, Qwill!" she protested. "That's tremendously

kind of you, but you should buy a new car for your-self."

"I insist, Polly. Go over to Gippel's and look at the new models. Pick out a color you like."

"Well, we'll argue about that when I return from Chicago. You can use the 'red job' while I'm away. What time do you want to pick me up Wednesday morning? I'll be staying in town at my sister-in-law's."

Feeling like a coward, he said, "Eight o'clock." Not only had he failed to resolve his dilemma, he had compounded it with his dastardly acquiescence.

SCENE NINE

Place: The Fitch mansion in West Middle Hummock

Time: A Tuesday Qwilleran would never forget

When Eddington Smith's old station wagon rumbled up to the carriage house Tuesday morning, Qwilleran went downstairs with the new picnic hamper.

"You didn't need to bring any food," the bookseller said. "I brought something for our lunch."

"It's not food," Qwilleran explained. "Koko is in

255

the hamper. I hope you don't object. I thought we could conduct an experiment to see if a cat can sniff out bookworms. If so, it would be a breakthrough for some scientific journal."

"I see," said Eddington with vague comprehension. Those were his last words for the next half hour. He was one of those intense drivers who are speechless while operating a vehicle. He gripped the wheel with whitened knuckles, leaned forward, and peered ahead in a trance, all the while stretching his lips in a joyless grin.

"My car flipped over in a ditch on Ittibittiwassee Road Sunday night, and it's totaled," Qwilleran said and waited for a sympathetic comment. There was no reaction from the mesmerized driver, so he continued.

"Fortunately I had my seat belt fastened, and I wasn't hurt except for a lump on my elbow as big as a golf ball and a stitch in my side, but the cats were thrown from the car. They disappeared in the woods. By the time I found them, they'd had an altercation with a skunk, and I had to drive them to the animal clinic. Did you ever spend fifteen minutes with two skunked animals in a car with the windows closed?"

There was no reply.

"I didn't dare roll the windows down more than an inch or two, because the cats were loose in the backseat, and I didn't know how wild they'd be after their experience. I couldn't breathe, Edd! I thought of stopping at the hospital for a shot of oxygen. Instead I just stepped on the gas and hoped I wouldn't turn blue."

Even this dramatic account failed to distract Eddington's concentration from the road.

"When I got home, I took a bath in tomato juice. Mr. O'Dell raided three grocery stores and bought every can they had on the shelf. He had to burn my clothes and the cats' coop. Their commodes were in the car when it flipped, and they rattled around like ice cubes in a cocktail shaker. One of them conked me on the head. I'm still combing gravel out of my hair and moustache."

Qwilleran peered into Eddington's face with concern. He was conscious, but that was all.

"The cats were deodorized at the clinic, but there's no guarantee it'll last. I may have to buy a gallon of Old Spice. I'm trying to keep them downwind."

After a while Qwilleran tired of hearing his own voice, and they drove in funereal silence until they reached the Fitch mansion. Eddington parked the car at the backdoor in a service yard enclosed by a high, stone wall.

If the murderers had parked there, Qwilleran observed, their vehicle would not have been visible from either of the approach roads; on the other hand, if they had stationed a lookout in the vehicle, he could not have seen David and Jill approaching. The lookout may have been patrolling the property with a walkie-talkie, he decided.

Eddington had a key to the back door, which led

into a large service hall—the place where Harley's body had been found. Doors opened into the kitchen, laundry, butler's pantry, and servants' dining room. Qwilleran was carrying the wicker hamper; Eddington was carrying a shopping bag, and after groping in its depths he produced a can of soup and two apples and left them on the kitchen table. Then he led the way to the Great Hall.

Although lighted by clerestory windows 30 feet overhead, the hall was a dismal conglomeration of primitive spears and shields, masks, drums, a canoe carved from a log, shrunken heads, and ceremonial costumes covered with dusty feathers. Qwilleran sneezed. "Where is the library?" he asked.

"I'll show you the drawing room and dining room first," Eddington said, opening large, double doors. These rooms were loaded with suits of armor, totem poles, stone dragons, medieval brasses, and stuffed monkeys in playful poses.

"Where are the books?" Qwilleran repeated.

Opening another great door Eddington said, "And this is the smoking room. Harley cleared it out and moved in some of his own things."

Qwilleran noted a ship's figurehead, carved and painted and seven feet tall, an enormous pilot wheel, a mahogany and brass binnacle, and an original print of the 1805 gunboat, signed, and obviously better than his reproduction. There were several sailing trophies. And on the mantel, on shelves and on tables there were model ships in glass cases.

The hamper that Qwilleran was clutching began to bounce and swing.

He said, "Koko is enthusiastic about nautical things. Would it be all right to let him out?"

Eddington nodded his pleasure and approval. " 'Enthusiasm is the fever of reason,' as Victor Hugo said."

It was the liveliest display of spirit that Koko had shown since his ordeal. He hopped out of the hamper and scampered to a two-foot replica of the HMS *Bounty*, a three-masted ship with intricate rigging and brass figurehead. Then he trotted to a fleet of three small ships: the *Niña*, the *Pinta*, and the *Santa Maria*, all under full sail with flags and pennants flying. When he discovered a nineteenth century gunboat with brass cannon, Koko rose on his hind legs, craning his neck and pawing the air.

"Now where's the library?" Qwilleran asked as he returned a protesting cat to the hamper.

It was a two-story room circled by a balcony, with books everywhere. Although there were no windows—and no daylight to damage the fine bindings—there were art-glass chandeliers that made the tooled leather sparkle like gold lace.

"How many of these do we have to dust?" Qwilleran wanted to know.

"I do a few hundred each time. I don't hurry. I enjoy handling them. Books like to be handled."

"You're a true bibliophile, Edd."

" 'In the highest civilization, the book is still the

highest delight.' That's what Emerson said, anyway."

"Emerson would have a hard time explaining that to the VCR generation. Let me close the doors and release Koko from his prison. He'll flip when he sees these books. He's a bibliophile himself."

Koko leaped from the hamper and surveyed the scene. On three walls there were banks of bookshelves alternating with sections of fine wood paneling, each with a curio cabinet containing small collectibles in disorganized array. There were Indian arrowheads and carved ivories, seashells and silver chalices, chunks of quartz and amethyst mixed with gold figurines that might have been smuggled from an Egyptian tomb. (Amanda had said a lot of them were fakes.) Above each cabinet was a mounted animal head or a gilded clock or an elaborate birdcage or a display of large bones like relics of some prehistoric age. Koko inventoried all of this, then discovered the spiral staircase, which he mounted cautiously. It was different from any of the staircases he had known.

Meanwhile, Eddington had pulled a bundle of clean rags from his shopping bag. "You can start in that corner with *S*. I left off at *R*. Slap the covers together gently, then wipe the head and sides with a cloth. Dust the shelf before you put the books back."

By this time Koko was whirling up and down the spiral stairs in a blur of pale fur and using the balcony as an indoor track.

Eddington opened the shallow drawer of the library table, a massive slab of oak supported by four carved gryphons. He removed the drawer entirely, and, after groping inside the cavity, brought out a key. "The rare books are in a locked room with the right temperature and humidity," he said. " 'Infinite riches in a little room,' as Marlowe said." Carrying his shopping bag he unlocked a door in a paneled wall and stepped inside. Qwilleran heard the lock click.

As he started dusting he pondered how much of Eddington's time in the locked room was spent with Cyrus Fitch's torrid literature. He himself had to exercise severe self-discipline to resist reading everything he dusted: Shaw, Shelley, Sheridan, for starters.

Koko busied himself here and there, and his activity and excitement caused his deodorant to lose its effectiveness. "Go and play at the other end of the room," Qwilleran told him. "Your BO is getting a little strong."

At noon Eddington reappeared and said somberly, "Time for lunch." He looked worried.

"Anything wrong in there, Edd?"

"There's a book missing."

"Valuable?"

The bookseller nodded. "There might be more missing. I won't know till I finish checking the whole inventory."

"Could I help you? Could I read off the listings or

anything like that?" Qwilleran had a great desire to see that room.

"No, I can do it better by myself. Do you like cream of chicken soup?"

Koko was now examining the far end of the room—the only wall without bookshelves. It was richly paneled, and it sealed off one end of the library under the balcony. Koko always discovered anything that was different, and this wall looked like an afterthought; it destroyed the symmetry of the room.

"Start heating the soup," Qwilleran said. "I want to finish dusting this bottom shelf."

As soon as Eddington had left, he rapped the odd wall with his knuckles. This had been a bootlegger's house, and bootleggers were known to like secret rooms and subterranean passages. He studied it for irregularities or hidden latches. He pressed the individual sections, hoping to find one less stable than the others. While he was systematically examining the wall, the library door opened.

"Soup's ready!"

"Beautiful paneling!" Qwilleran said. "Just by touching it anyone could tell it's superior to the stuff they use nowadays."

He bundled Koko into the hamper, apologizing for his scent, although Eddington insisted he didn't notice anything, and the three of them went to the kitchen for lunch.

"It isn't much," the little man said, "but 'We must eat to live and live to eat.' Fielding said that."

"You are exceptionally well-read," said Qwilleran. "I suspect you do more reading than dusting when you disappear into that little room. What kind of books do you have in there?"

The bookseller's face brightened. "*The Nuremberg Chronicle, 1493* . . . a Bay psalm book in perfect condition—the first book published in the English colonies in America . . . a first of Poe's "Tamerlane" . . . the first bible printed in America; it's in an Indian language."

"What are they worth?"

"Some of them could bring a price in five or six figures!"

"If one were stolen, would it be difficult to sell? Are there fences who handle hot books?"

"I don't know. I never thought about that."

"Which book is missing?"

"An early work on anatomy—very rare."

"A family member may have borrowed it to read," Qwilleran suggested.

"I don't think so. It's in Latin."

"I'm amazed at your knowledge of books, Edd. I wish I could remember everything I've read and come up with a trenchant quote for every occasion."

Eddington looked guilty. "I haven't done much reading," he confessed. "I took Winston Churchill's advice. He said: 'It's a good thing for an uneducated man to read books of quotations.' "

After the meagre lunch (Koko had a few bits of chicken from the soup) the party returned to the library. Eddington locked himself in the little room while Qwilleran resumed his dusting (Tennyson, Thackeray, Twain) and Koko resumed his explorations.

The hush in the library was almost unnerving. Qwilleran could hear himself breathe. He could hear Koko padding across the parquet floor. He could hear . . . a sudden creaking of wood at the far end of the room. Koko was standing on his hind legs and resting his paws on the paneled wall that was different from the others. A section of it was moving, swinging open. Koko hopped through the aperture.

Qwilleran hurried to the spot. "Koko, get out of there!" he scolded, but the inspector general had found something new to inspect and was totally deaf. The secret door opened into a storage room—windowless, airless, stifling, and dark. Qwilleran groped for a light switch but found none. In the half-light slanting in from the library chandeliers he could see ghostly forms in the shadows: life-size figures of marble or carved wood, a huge Buddha, crude pottery ornamented with grotesque faces, a steel safe, and . . . a brass bugle! It was the one he would have used in the Theatre Club production if the show had not been canceled, and he resisted the impulse to shatter the silence with a brassy blast.

In the close atmosphere Koko's unfortunate aroma was accentuated. He was prowling in and out of the shadows, and one of the items that attracted him was an attaché case. Qwilleran had learned not to take Koko's discoveries casually, and he grabbed the case away from the purring cat. Kneeling on the floor in a patch of dim light he snapped the latches, opened the lid eagerly, and sucked in his breath at the sight of its contents. As he did so, a shadow fell across the open case, and he looked up to see the silhouette of a man in the doorway—a man with a club.

Lunging for the bugle, Qwilleran raised it to his lips and blew a deafening blast. At the same moment the man came through the door, swinging the club. Qwilleran bellowed and struck at him with the bugle. In the semidarkness both weapons missed their mark. The club descended again, and Qwilleran ducked. He swung the bugle again with both hands, like a ballbat, but connected with nothing. The two men were flailing blindly and wildly. Qwilleran was breathing hard, and the stitch in his side felt like a knife-thrust.

Dodging behind a cigar store Indian he waited for the right moment and slashed again with all his strength. He missed the man, but he struck the club. To his amazement it crumbled! Instantly he swung the brass bugle at his assailant's head, and the man sank dizzily to the floor.

Only then did Qwilleran see his face in full light. *"David!"* he shouted.

Outside the door a hollow voice roared, "Stop or I'll shoot!"

Qwilleran froze and slowly raised his hands.

From the corner of his eye he could see a handgun; it was pointed at the crumpled figure on the floor.

"Edd! Where'd you get that?" he gasped.

"It was in my shopping bag," said the little man, reverting to his usual shy delivery. For the first time in his life he had projected his voice.

"Keep him covered while I call the police, Edd. He might come around and start trouble again."

As he spoke, Koko emerged from the shadows and stalked the supine figure on the floor. He was purring mightily as he rubbed his head against the sprawled legs. He climbed on the man's chest and sniffed nose to nose. The man stirred and opened his eyes, saw two blue eyes staring into his own, caught a whiff of Koko's aroma, and passed out again.

SCENE
TEN

Place: Back at Qwilleran's apartment over
      the garage
Time: Later the same day

No one talked on the way back to Pickax.
Eddington Smith was frozen to the wheel; Qwilleran
was still aghast at his recent discovery; and Koko
was asleep in the hamper, which was placed at the
extreme rear of the station wagon, with all the windows open.

"Thanks for the ride, Edd. Thanks for the good
lunch," Qwilleran said when they arrived. "Don't

forget to report that missing book to the law-yer."

"Oh, I found it! It was on the wrong shelf!"

"Well, it was an exciting afternoon, to put it mildly."

" 'Excitement is the drunkenness of the spirit,' as somebody said."

"Uh . . . yes. I'm glad you didn't have to use your gun."

"I am, too," said Eddington. "I didn't have any bullets."

It was then that Qwilleran noticed Francesca's car in the drive, and it reminded him that his troubles were not over. He carried the hamper into the ga-rage. "Sorry, Koko. I've got to keep you down here until Fran leaves. You're smelling pretty ripe."

As he climbed the stairs to his apartment, his nose told him that Yum Yum also needed another shot of deodorant spray, and his eyes notified him that something was missing in the hallway. The Mackin-tosh coat of arms was not leaning against the wall in its accustomed place.

"Hello!" he called. "Fran, are you here?"

When there was no reply, he checked the prem-ises. In the living room, lying in the middle of the floor, was the heavy circle of ornamental iron. In the cats' apartment he found Yum Yum huddled in a corner, with a pathetic expression in her violet-blue eyes. In his studio he found a red light glowing on the answer-box. He punched a button, listened to the message and then hurriedly called Francesca at home.

"Qwill, you'll never believe what happened!" she said. "I wanted to incorporate the Mackintosh thing in one of your radiator enclosures, so I went over to measure it and see how it would look. I was half-way across the living room with it . . ."

"You *lifted* that piece of iron?"

"No, I was rolling it like a hoop when I accidentally stepped on a cat, and it screeched like seven devils. I was so spooked that I rolled the damn thing over my foot!"

"Yum Yum's screech could raise the dead," he said. "I hope you're not hurt, Fran."

"Hurt! I was wearing sandals and broke three toes! A police car took me to the hospital. Dad will pick up my car later. But Qwill," she wailed, "I won't be able to go to Chicago tomorrow!"

Qwilleran heaved a sigh of relief that activated the stitch in his side, but he extended sympathy and said all the right things. After that he went to the cats' apartment, picked up Yum Yum and stroked her smelly fur. "Sweetheart," he said, "did you trip her accidentally, or did you know what you were doing?"

Immediately he telephoned Polly at the library to remind her that he was driving her to the airport in the morning. "I may board the plane with you," he added. "I know some good restaurants in Chicago."

He sprayed the cats and was serving them a small shrimp cocktail and a dish of veal Stroganoff when he happened to glance out the front window. A police car was in the driveway, and the burly figure of the chief was stepping out of the passenger's door and approaching Francesca's car with a bunch of keys.

Qwilleran opened the window. "Brodie! Come on up for a cup of coffee!"

The chief was more amiable than he had been when questioned about the Fitch case. He clomped up the stairs saying, "I hope it's not the same witch's brew you gave me once before."

Qwilleran locked the cats in their apartment, set the automatic coffeemaker for extra strong, and handed the chief a mug. "You're in a better frame of mind than the last time I saw you."

"Arrgh!" growled Brodie.

"Is that a comment on the coffee or the state investigation?"

"The case is settled now, looks like. So maybe I can talk without getting in hot water. That evidence you found in the closet cracked it wide open. It was the kind of evidence they were hoping for."

"You don't need to repeat this, but ... it was Koko who found it! First, he discovered how to get into the secret closet."

"What did I tell you? I told you we could use him on the force."

"I never did buy the Chipmunk theory, and when I opened the attaché case, I knew it was an inside job. I figured that David had killed Harley, rifled the safe, and stashed the money and jewels and murder weapon in the closet, intending to pick it up later. That was a lot of cash for a banker to have in the house."

Brodie nodded. "The bank examiners are in town. They'll find a few shortages, I'll bet."

"I didn't know who it was when he attacked me in the dark storage room, but I knew I was fighting for my life. He had killed twice, and I had found the evidence. After I stunned him with his grandfather's bugle, I began to collect my wits, and I thought, Why would David kill his twin? What possible motive? At that moment Koko walked over to him, purring like a helicopter. When he sniffed the guy's moustache, I said to myself, That's not David on the floor; that's Harley." Qwilleran paused and caressed his moustache with satisfaction. "Koko could smell the spirit gum! The moustache was false—glued on the guy's upper lip."

"YOW!" came a stentorian cheer from down the hall.

"He knows we're talking about him," said Qwilleran.

Brodie said, "So you think you know the motive now?"

"I'm pretty sure. From what I've heard on the Pickax grapevine I've constructed a scenario. See if you think it'll play:

"Scene 1: Margaret Fitch, a manipulative mother, encourages David to marry Harley's girl, while Harley is serving time in prison for criminally negligent homicide.

"Scene 2: Harley returns home and marries a tramp to spite David, Jill, and his meddlesome parent.

"Scene 3: Harley is still carrying the torch for Jill, however, and she realizes she's still in love with him. They can't afford to divorce their mates because Margaret dominates them with an iron fiscal policy. She gives them a taste for luxuries but keeps them poor.

"Scene 4: Jill plots the embezzlement of bank funds, the murders, and Harley's exchange of identities with his twin.

"Scene 5: On the night of the murder David and Jill arrive at Harley's house at 6:30 as usual. Harley has already shot Belle, and he turns the gun on his brother. Then he exchanges their jewelry and wallets—and shaves off David's moustache. Meanwhile, Jill is staging the ransacking of the library and bedroom, packing the attaché case with money, jewels, and the murder weapon.

"Scene 6: Despite Harley's acting talent and his false moustache, his parents know he isn't David. His mother has a fatal stroke, and his father can't face the choice he has to make—either to inform the police that his son has been murdered by his twin brother, or to become an accessory after the fact and live with a heinous secret.

"Scene 7: Harley and Jill plan to disappear in South America, but their getaway is foiled."

The chief grinned and shook his head. "Even

Lieutenant Hames won't believe the one about the cat and the glued-on moustache."

When the news of the showdown at the Fitch mansion leaked out, the Pickax grapevine worked overtime, and Qwilleran's phone rang all evening.

Arch Riker said, "We're remaking page one for tomorrow's paper, but there's one statement from Edd Smith that won't wash. He says you were hit on the head with a club and it shattered. We all know you're a hardhead, Qwill, but even *your* skull isn't hard enough to shatter a club."

"It wasn't a club, Arch. It looked like the thighbone of a camel. It was one of the bizarre relics on display in the library. There we were—in a dark closet—lunging at each other like Hamlet and Laertes, only those guys had rapiers, and all we had was a bone and a brass bugle. We must have looked like a couple of baggy-pants comics. When I whacked the bone with the bugle, it crumbled, and I realized it was made of plaster. Amanda says they have a lot of fakes in that place."

When Amanda herself called, she growled, "This whole stink wouldn't have happened if that family hadn't been so damned stingy with their money—and so phony about everything! Mr. and Mrs. Perfect, they thought they were! And they conned the whole county into believing it."

Gary Pratt also telephoned. "Jeez! I'm glad it's over. I probably knew more about Harley than anybody else did, sailing with him all the time. When he came home from his year in the clink, he was full of hate. He couldn't forgive David for stealing his woman."

Pete Parrott's message was brief. "I hope that SOB gets what he deserves!"

Roger MacGillivray, who had written the breaking story on the murder, said, "You know, Qwill, if it's true that Jill planned it all, she had a neat script—almost too neat. The plumbing emergency . . . the vehicle going fast down the dirt road and throwing up a cloud of dust . . . all those convincing details!"

Polly Duncan was the last to call. "Your phone has been busy all evening, Qwill. Are the rumors true? How did you know it was Harley and not David?"

"It started at my birthday party, Polly. Koko took an instant liking to Harley, Edd Smith, and Wally Toddwhistle—and later, my paperhanger. This theory may sound farfetched, but . . . they were all men who regularly worked with adhesives, and Koko is a fiend for glue. When he saw Harley's model ships, he pranced on his hind legs like the Mackintosh cat. And at the Fitch library, when he showed such an avid interest in the man on the floor, I knew it wasn't David."

Late that night, when the freight train whistled at crossings north of town, Qwilleran sprawled on the sofa and reviewed the events of the last two weeks. Yum Yum was asleep on his chest, and Koko was balancing on the back of the sofa.

"Why were you so interested in sea stories all of a sudden?" Qwilleran asked him. "Why did you keep tilting the gunboat picture? Did you sense the identity of the murderer? Were you trying to steer my attention to a sailor and builder of model ships?"

Koko opened his mouth in a wide yawn, all teeth and pink gullet. It was, after all, 2:30 A.M., and he had had a hard day.

"Was it a coincidence that you and Yum Yum started acting like bookends? Or were you pointing a paw at the *twins*?"

Koko squeezed his eyes sleepily. He was sitting tall but swaying slightly. He almost toppled off the sofa back.

"You rogue! You pretend you haven't the slightest idea what I'm talking about," Qwilleran said. "We'll try it once more . . . Would you like some turkey?"

Koko's eyes popped open, and Yum Yum raised her head abruptly. With one accord the two of them jumped to the floor, yikking and squealing as they raced to the refrigerator, where Qwilleran found them arranged in identical poses, like twins, as they stared up at the door handle.

EPILOGUE

The prosecutor is seeking a change of venue for the trial of Harley and Jill, arguing that it will be impossible to seat an objective jury in Moose County, where the citizenry is still under the spell of the Fitch mystique.

According to Jill, who is cooperating with investigators to save her own neck, they staged the vandalism at the dental clinic to destroy the twins' dental records.

Qwilleran no longer employs the services of Francesca Brodie, and Yum Yum has reverted to her fastidious habits in the commode.

The Siamese, using their own built-in deodorant applied with long pink tongues, have dispelled the memory of the black-and-white kitty on Ittibitti-wassee Road.

Qwilleran is reading *Moby-Dick* aloud to the cats and spending weekends at Polly Duncan's cozy house in the country.

The Klingenschoen Theatre will open with an original revue written by Qwilleran and Hixie Rice. The hit number is sure to be "I Left My Heart in Pickax City."

Koko is learning how to turn the television off.

FINAL CURTAIN